THE LAST TEACHER

MACKENZIE AUGUST PREQUEL

ALAN LEE

The Last Teacher
Written by Alan Lee

Printed in USA
Copyright © 2015 by Alan Janney

Cover by Inspired Cover Designs
Formatting by Polgarus

Paperback ISBN:
9780998316512

Sign up for my newsletter here. I alert you about my releases, and always offer new books at a discount for my email list.

Sparkle Press

❀ Created with Vellum

For Sarah
because you are so pretty

1

"Why do you want to be an English teacher, Mr. August?" The question came from Principal Martin. Her hair was back in a hasty bun, she wore no makeup, and she was apparently too no-nonsense to waste time on smiling. I liked her.

"I worked at a church previously and I was awful at it," I replied. We sat in her small office, walled in by overflowing bookshelves. "But I liked the teaching."

"You look too big to be a pastor."

"And too handsome," I said. Her eyebrow arched and she remained quiet. Perhaps she was blind. "I wasn't a pastor. I worked with the youth group."

"Why did you leave that job?"

"I cursed in the pulpit a few times. Huge no-no."

She laughed, slightly, as did one of the other three women in the office. The young, cute one. Really cute. The other two did not laugh. Perhaps they were deaf.

"That's a deal breaker for God?" the principal asked.

"Not necessarily for God."

"Your resume says you used to be a police officer," said one of the older women in the room, reading over a paper through her bifocals. "Why did you leave that job?"

"A cornucopia of reasons. Bottom line, I needed a change."

"Were you good at that job?" the Principal asked.

"Extremely."

"Why do you want to be an English teacher?" she asked again.

"I partially put myself through college as a long-term substitute English teacher, and enjoyed it. And no one will shoot at me. Or point out that I'm bad at church."

"I'm not good at church either," she said. "We've been interviewing all week and still don't think we've found the eighth-grade teacher that we need. We even interviewed in-house. SOL scores were down last year. We're looking for a strong teacher to bring them back up."

"I am *really* strong."

"This would be a weird hire."

"Yet, a good one."

"I must admit, it'd be nice to have a former police officer around. I mean, in addition to our resource officer, who is..." She trailed off with a pained wince. "We think our school is haunted."

"Haunted," I said. "The Ghost of Christmas Break?"

"I'm joking about the ghost. But we've suffered a series of things we can't explain, like our stuff being moved, doors left open, misplaced items. Things like that. Nothing major. Do not let that deter you, however."

"I'm undeterred. Sounds like kids playing jokes."

"More likely a nosey staff member. But we can't catch him."

"Or her. You sexist," I said.

"You'd be part of a team with these three women. The four of you will teach the core subjects to the same one hundred students. These teachers' opinion of you is very important in making this decision," she said.

"I'm eager to please."

"Who has questions for Mr. August?"

The two older women had both been teaching for over twenty years and interviews were old news to them. Other than being slightly amused at my size and former occupations, they lost interest in me after I satisfied their professional grilling.

The younger, dark brown-haired teacher was one year out of college and willing to be friendly. "Why South Hill?" she asked.

"I posted my resume yesterday. Ms. Martin called me this morning and asked me to drive down. If I'm hired, I'll cancel the other interviews I made on the way here. Otherwise, I'll drive around Virginia for interviews until someone hires me."

"You have an unusual accent."

"Louisiana roots," I replied.

"You sound like Harry Connick Jr."

"Lucky him."

"What's your first name?"

"Mackenzie," I said.

"Do people call you Mack?"

"Most everyone."

"So you don't care where you end up?"

"As long as it's someplace new," I said. "I'm looking for a change."

"South Hill is tiny. There's not much to do around here."

"The county website claims excellent golf and fishing. What else is there?"

"You play golf?" Principal Martin interrupted.

"Poorly, yes."

Principal Martin kicked me out so the four of them could talk about me behind my back. I sat in the office waiting room and did my best to be oblivious to the suggestive looks I was getting from the guidance office secretary. Five minutes later the three teachers walked out and passed me. Two of them nodded politely and kept walking. The youngest paused to rest her hand on my shoulder, and her pinky brushed my neck.

"I'll help you get started." She smiled. She winked. And she left.

The principal walked out without a smile.

"If you'll be the golf coach, you're hired."

"Done." Free golf.

"Tomorrow's Friday. You start then. Kids arrive Monday. Think you can handle that?"

"As long as the kids don't bring guns, I'm great."

"Welcome to South Hill Middle School."

AFTER A BRIEF TOUR of the school, including a stop by my classroom, I told the principal I'd see her tomorrow. I walked to my car and stopped just before reaching the door.

My car was unlocked. I never leave my car open, and yet I could clearly see the popped lock through the glass. I opened the door without using the key and slid in. The glove compartment was open. My pistol was still there.

Pistol, registration, flashlight, service records...all still within the compartment. Nothing seemed to be missing.

Who'd want to break into my car and not take anything? Had I left my car locked? I knew I had. Local police? Neighborhood kid with a Slim Jim?

The nosey staff member?

If I had enough time over the next twenty-four hours I might dust it for prints out of curiosity, but I doubted it. Nothing was taken.

2

-Thirty-nine days until the first body is discovered

I spent the night at a local hotel. I woke up, bought breakfast and a change of clothes at Wal-Mart, and went to work. No one had broken into my car, which was nice.

The classroom I'd been given was actually a large trailer beside the school. Several other trailers squatted with mine in a semicircle surrounding one of the school's exits. I unlocked mine and went in. Principal Martin arrived soon after.

"The teacher you're replacing told me she was quitting just over a week ago. She took everything with her, including school property. That explains why this room is pathetic as hell."

"Hey, I didn't make fun of your office."

"Do the best you can with what you have. We'll give you a small redecorating budget in addition to your supply allowance. Open house begins at noon." The principal paused to evaluate me. "Gosh, you're a big man," she said on her way out, closing the door behind her.

I spent the next few hours rearranging the classroom. After disentangling the pile of twenty-three desks, I pointed them as closely as possible to the dry-erase board in the corner of the room. Beside the dry-erase board I planted the old wooden podium and the older swivel stool. I made a small fort in the back of the room with three small tables that'd serve as my desk.

It looked like a real classroom. I wondered if I looked like a real teacher.

Teachers came to introduce themselves and brought me posters I could hang up. Apparently students didn't learn until the student/poster ratio was met.

Taylor, the young brunette knockout from my interview, stopped by with a handwritten list of suggestions to prepare me for my first day. Somehow, I hadn't caught her last name the day before. She thought I sounded like Harry Connick Jr.

"It's an improvement," she said, looking at my trailer with mild disapproval. "I guess."

"I've already applied to be on the TLC special *Pimp My Classroom*," I said, and crossed my fingers for good luck. She laughed. Those had to be porcelain veneers. No one has teeth that perfect.

"I'm in the trailer next door."

"You're out here in the trailer park?"

"I prefer trailer quad. Somehow it validates my four year degree."

"Prestigious."

"Last year, some asshole spray painted 'Ms. Williams is trailer trash' on the side."

"Taylor Williams," I said, and cocked a brow.

"Yes, I know it sounds like a news anchor."

"I didn't say anything."

"I have two last names, get over it."

"Way over it," I said.

"Good. Where are you staying?"

"Hotel near the interstate."

"Switch to the bed and breakfast downtown. It's cheaper and nicer," she said.

"By downtown, do you mean the immediate vicinity surrounding the single stoplight?"

She pointed at me on her way out of the room. "Don't make fun of my hometown, and I'll be really nice to you." The door closed behind her. Never make fun of South Hill. Because those were elite legs.

My next visitors were both seventh grade teachers. Ms. Friedmond and Mr. Cannon. Mr. Cannon brought me a few posters. He taught seventh grade English. He was very thin, and had shaggy blonde hair and a thin goatee. He wore glasses, and a short sleeved white button up shirt. I hated those. But still, it was nice to see another guy teacher. Mental note to stop by his room and see how another man had decorated his English classroom. He had a classroom, not a trailer. I bet he thought himself superior.

Ms. Friedmond said, "How about church? Found one here yet?"

"Not in the past twenty-four hours, no."

"Well, hey, we've got a real nice place over at Chase Baptist. You should come check us out. Real nice," Cannon said.

Friedmond nodded. She looked sassy. I liked her.

"You're a big guy," Mr. Cannon said, hands in pockets and rocking on his heels. "Play football? In college?"

"I did, but we were a juggernaut of terrible."

"Where?"

"Radford University."

"I didn't know they had a football team."

"Ouch."

"Have you found a place to live?" Mrs. Friedmond asked. "I got a spare bedroom. I'll make popcorn. We'll watch Netflix."

"You're naughty, Ms. Friedmond."

"Offer stands."

"I haven't started looking."

"Well, great. If you're interested, our church is renting out its parsonage. Real nice place." Cannon pulled out his business card and handed it over. The letters were glossy and stood up from the card. Fancy pants. "That's my number, just in case. I designed the card myself. Something of a computer whiz. I'd be happy to help set up your computer. Anyway, I can have the church contact you about the parsonage."

"Tell you what. As soon as I get situated I'll contact you for your church's number."

"Do that." He nodded. "Do that. And I'll give you directions."

Despite being a showoff, I liked Mr. Cannon. Eager and friendly.

Mrs. Ballard came in a few minutes later, with my handbook and various papers to sign. I had already lost track of teachers, but she reminded me I was on her "team." I signed things she told me to sign until the door opened and my eight-month-old son entered the room, carried by his grandfather.

My son was one of those babies who came out perfect and looked like he could make a fortune modeling baby clothes or food or diapers. Big blue eyes, a hint of hazel. Front teeth coming in. Still not much hair. That was getting embarrassing.

He came close to hyperventilating at seeing me. I took him, greeted Timothy August (my father), and introduced Mrs. Ballard.

"I didn't know you had a son," she cooed over him, her professionalism melting. Love at first sight.

"He stayed with his grandfather for a few days while I traveled."

"What's his name?"

"Kix."

"He's adorable," she said.

"He gets it from his mother."

"Is she moving here too?" she asked.

"She died in childbirth."

"I'm so sorry," she gasped. "I didn't know you were a widower."

"I'm not. She wasn't my wife."

"Oh...forgive me." She stumbled through her nerves. "I keep forgetting girls don't mind getting pregnant out of wedlock these days."

"She *was* married. To my best friend."

Speechless. Strike three. You're out. My father shook his head. He hated when I didn't tell the whole story. Kix patted my face affectionately.

"I told you I was a terrible youth pastor."

3

-Thirty-six days until the first body is discovered -

I arrived at school thirty minutes before the buses were scheduled to roll in. I wore modern brown Sketchers, khakis, brown belt, blue button-up and a red tie. South Hill is hot. My sleeves were rolled up.

Teachers are required to sign in, so the office will know to make emergency sub calls if a signature is missing. I went to the office, nodded good mornings and signed in. My mailbox read, "New English Teacher." I chose not to make a scene my first day, so I gathered the attendance folder and went to my trailer.

Someone had been there before me.

My door locked two ways. A quick lock that sprung open when the inside handle turned and a permanent setting that would keep the door locked until intentionally disengaged. I had left the lock on its permanent setting, but when I entered the lock immediately clicked free.

In other words, someone had been in here with a key.

I scanned the room, only mildly intrigued. Nothing in the room was worth stealing. Curious. The trash can was spilling over a little, just like I'd left it on Friday, so the intruder wasn't the custodian. Nothing new was waiting for me on my desk.

First, my car. Now, my classroom.

The principal had been right - our school had a busy little bee. And the bee kept breaking into my stuff.

My door opened with ten minutes to go before the start of school and in walked a bald, black man wearing a tie with "I Love Jesus" written on it a hundred times. He was fifty, give or take.

"Howdy," I said.

"Morning," he said. "I'm Mr. Charlie."

"Howdy Mr. Charlie."

"I heard you were a pastor."

"Youth pastor. Kinda. Really bad at it."

"We have something in common."

He smiled.

Ah jeez. He was a pastor. I didn't like other pastors. I decline to comment.

"I'm a preacher too. You see, I used to be a correctional officer," he said. He spoke like a preacher. His words were heavy with significance and brief dramatic pauses. Sincerity, however, was evident. "And I got tired of seeing boys coming through past the age of saving. I decided to come here and save as many as I could."

After living in California almost a decade, the Bible Belt required some adjustment. Christians everywhere.

"I teach art," he said. "And I am a substitute bus driver. The office need a sub, they call me first. These kids, see, they need teachers. But they also need people like us. Like you and me, you see. These kids need an education but they also need saving. And that's really why I'm here."

"Where do you preach?"

"All over," he said, and waved his hand around vaguely. "A church need me, they call. I was only ordained last year."

"Sort of a bus driver sub *and* preacher sub?"

"Yeah." He smiled. He liked that. I'm a riot. "Yeah, something like that."

Mr. Charlie was my homeroom helper. As middle schoolers began filing in a few minutes later, he signed them up for lockers and collected money. He informed me that he wouldn't be staying long because he had an art class to get ready for.

Eighth graders are social. They have to be. It's that stage of life, and to expect otherwise is ridiculous. So I let them talk until the bell rang to start class. I took a deep breath to begin my illustrious career as an educator only to have Mr. Charlie intercept the class on his way out of the room.

"Before I leave," he told them, "I want to share something with you, students. Me and Mr. August, we both have something in common." He placed one hand on his chest and held the other one in my direction. Uh-oh. I had a bad feeling I knew what was coming. If I could get away with it, I might have punched Mr. Charlie in the back of his bald head to shut him up. I'd decided not to tell my students I used to work at a church. "We're both ministers," he said, with a fair amount of dignity. "So you have to treat us with respect. I seen you at church when you have on your good behavior, and I expect you to act that way with Mr. August." He stared at them for a long moment, before turning to look at me. "I have to get to my class. You okay here, Mr. August?"

"Super," I sighed. My secret didn't last past homeroom.

4

-Thirty-six days until the first body is discovered -

Third and fourth periods rolled around. Two back-to-back planning periods. Heaven. I sat behind my desk and put my feet up. Not bad so far. The students hadn't discovered I had no idea what I was doing, and I liked them. But it was the first day, and I imagined the crazies didn't come out until at least the third day.

My door opened and in walked a cute, blonde teacher I'd seen once before.

"Hi," she said.

"Hello blonde teacher."

"I'm Kristen," she said, walking into the room. She looked like a teacher. Stylish but severe. Key hanging around her neck from the South Hill Middle School lanyard. She looked too young to be a mom but I was getting a mother vibe.

"I'm Mack," I said.

"I'm new too. I thought we should be friends."

A thought occurred to me. Every face was new to me, so I had been automatically assuming all other teachers were old friends. I was wrong.

"How new?" I asked and stood to shake her hand.

"I was hired two weeks before you, so I'm older. And I also went to Radford University."

"No kidding," I said.

"For graduate school. I did undergrad at William and Mary."

"You're smarter than me. I get it."

That got a laugh. I'm hilarious.

"When did you graduate?" she asked.

I told her.

"Ah. I just graduated this spring with Secondary Education."

"Shucks," I said. "We can't play the 'Do you know...?' game."

"Ready for this? My husband and I have an eight-month-old daughter."

"I have a son that age," I said.

"I know."

"We're almost the same person."

"Except I'm smarter." She beamed.

"And a stalker, apparently."

"How's that?" she asked.

"You know everything about me."

"You're new," she shrugged. "People talk."

"You're new too."

"Yeah but you're new and scary. People aren't sure if they can talk to you yet. I'm cute. They trust me," she said.

"I'm cute."

She tilted her head, considering, and said, "Yeah, you are, but scary cute. Not the same. Plus, I grew up here."

"Is that so?" I mused. "Then perhaps you could recommend a good local daycare."

"I would recommend a sweet old lady who is watching my daughter, Jessica, and another kid, and she is willing to take on one more before she stops advertising."

"That's perfect."

"I know," she said.

"Serendipitous, even."

"Quite."

"If you're joking, it's not funny," I said. "She sounds too perfect."

"I'm not joking."

"I'm scary, remember? Don't play with me."

"I'll get you her number."

5

-Thirty-five days until the first body is discovered -

Taylor had been right. The bed and breakfast was indeed a nicer place to stay. The kind of place that felt like an expensive house with the large, elaborate master bedroom all to yourself. Egyptian cotton sheets, white down comforter, poster bed, full bath, mints on the pillow, the whole nine yards. Plus a baby. And his grandfather.

Kix bounced on my father's knee and talked in a language whose primary word involved sticking his tongue out several times. My father was cooing back and telling me how to impress principals. I had just hung up with Leta High, the nice lady who'd begin watching Kix tomorrow while I was at work. Life was good.

Someone knocked at the door.

"Expecting company?" Timothy August asked. He was the principal of an elementary school in Roanoke, Virginia and would be leaving soon to drive back tonight.

"Negative," I said and opened the door.

Taylor. The good-looking brunette in the trailer quad. She was dressed in heels, a skirt that could have passed for a scarf and a loosely buttoned white shirt. She was tan and her muscles were firm from exercise. Her brown hair framed her face in soft layers. She smiled at me and raised her eyebrows.

"Hi Mack. I see you took my advice," she said.

"Solid advice," I said. As far as looks went, she ranked in the top one percent. My chest tightened.

"I brought you a welcome basket." She held up an actual woven basket covered with a red checkered blanket. "May I come in?" Before I could answer, Kix made a noise and Taylor's eyes grew wide. "Oh shit, you have company?"

"I do," I said again. "Come in and meet part of my family."

She walked in hesitantly. My father smiled, trying to hide his amusement.

"This is my son, Kix."

"You have a kid?" she asked, sounding almost offended.

"I do. And a father. Timothy August. That's him right there, holding my kid."

My father introduced himself, set Kix down and said, "Time for me to go."

"No, no," Taylor said and turned for the door. "I'm leaving. I just came by to drop off the basket. Can't stay. I'm on my way home. See you tomorrow. Nice to meet you," she called as she retreated to the safety of the hallway and closed the door behind her.

My father looked at the basket, inside of which a bottle of wine was showing, and cocked an eyebrow at me.

"Nice work, son. I'm proud of you."

"Dad," I scolded him.

6

-Thirty-three days until the first body is discovered

I found a cabin for rent on Lake Gaston through the internet. The owners lived in Ohio and hadn't had much success renting the cabin during the previous year's off-season so they were looking for permanent tenants, rather than just the occasional weekend renter. I emailed and told them my situation and that I'd call the next day, which I did during my planning period. We worked out a rental price. I picked Kix up after school, drove down to the lake and found the cabin. The hidden key was exactly where the owners promised it'd be. I walked in, set Kix down, punched their number into my cell and told them I'd take it.

The cabin had three big bedrooms located in the back of the house. Also located on the main floor were both a kitchen and a living room, near the front door. Plenty of room for Kix to crawl around. If he ever learned. Downstairs was a garage and an unfinished area furnished with only a television and couch. A wooden walkway led to the dock one hundred feet behind the deck. The rent was less than my one-bedroom apartment had been when I'd lived in

LA. Definitely worth the twenty-minute drive to and from school. I wondered if Taylor would be willing to make the trip to surprise me.

I'm worth it.

-Twenty-eight days until the first body is discovered-

The local golf course let South Hill golf teams practice for free. My eagerness to play golf dimmed slightly when I discovered that the course had only nine holes. I was a long way from LA. The high school team had already been practicing for a week when we showed up for our first. Standing on the driving range, I surveyed both teams. The varsity team all wore khaki or plaid shorts, golf shoes and socks, golfing polo shirts, and hats with the proper golf endorsements. They stood tall and took smooth, fluid practice swings. The middle school team, however, was short, poorly dressed, and dug up impressive divots with their choppy hacks. My heart warmed to them. Gotta start sometime.

The varsity team moved off to begin a practice round. Their coach nodded at me. I nodded back. He had a mustache. I had a cooler golf visor. We tied.

"Gentlemen," I said to the team of seven short middle school boys. "Harken to me." I knew four of them from my classes. The other three looked like sixth or seventh graders. I bet I looked ancient to them.

"What's harken mean, Mr. August?" The question came from Stephen, a likable wiseass in my fifth period. He was a strong student. Like some other boys his age, his face didn't quite fit yet, his arms were too big for his body, and he didn't know what to do with his brown hair. He used his intelligence to coast by and make quasi-witty comments in the classroom. On the golf course, however, he looked lost.

"It means get over here." The seven piled in front of me, smaller ones moving quicker. "Welcome to golf, boys. I am thrilled you're here, and you're going to be ecstatic I'm here. Because I'm awesome. If you don't believe me, ask the others. I'm awesome."

"He always talks like this," another boy, Matt, said. Matt wore golfing gear. I'd met his father, who'd also been wearing golfing gear. Maybe he could loan Stephen some.

"We are going to have a great season. For those of you who don't know much about golf, you're going to learn. For those of you who do, you're going to get better. You can call me Coach or Coach August. Except for Matt, who has to call me Mr. August, or Your Honor. We're going to have a great season."

"You already said that," Stephen said.

"We're going to have a great season," I said again. "First, tell me your names."

After they told me their names and I came up with mnemonic nicknames, like Smart Guy Stephen or Mashed-Up Matt or Tiger Tom, we walked to the first tee. I could tell at least one of the younger guys didn't have a clue. Maybe none of them did. So we went over basics, like how to keep score, who gets to hit first, which tee box to use, how to use a tee, etc. As a team we played the course, taking turns hitting, looking over the greens, discussing how we should putt, and evaluating on the next tee box.

Everyone kept their own scorecard. I didn't write down numbers on my card. Instead I kept notes on the different guys and what they needed to work on. The younger guys had obvious fundamentals to get down and I could help with that, but I was going to let the course pro give the older, better golfers a few pointers. I could coach the team, but had no experience tweaking swings.

At the end of practice everyone left, including Stephen, whose mom came to pick him up in an old Pontiac. I went to go spy on the varsity coach and see what a real coach does.

-Twenty days until the first body is discovered-

"Mr. August, are you single?" Ms. Friedmond asked. She was the science teacher within my team. She had short hair, a great smile, and just enough cheerfulness to take the edge off her attitude.

I was sitting in the small teachers' workroom eating doughnuts with Mr. Cannon, the shaggy-haired seventh-grade English teacher; Kristen Short, the eighth-grade reading teacher who helped me find a sitter for Kix; and Ms. Friedmond. Teachers have terrible diets. Awful. Every other day someone else tries to be friendly and bring in sweets. I wouldn't be surprised to discover teachers eat worse than cops.

"Hard to believe, isn't it?" I said, and decided against flexing.

"Not that hard," she said. I should have flexed. Dang. "You're *scary* good-looking," she said.

Kristen hit the table lightly and said, "That's what I told him. He's scary looking."

"Where's your baby momma?" Ms. Friedmond asked.

"No longer with us," I said.

"Single widower with a young baby, teaching English," Ms. Friedmond said. "I'm getting excited just thinking about it. You're white, I'm black, and I don't care."

"Thinking about it makes me tired, not excited," I said, and picked out a doughnut with chocolate frosting and sprinkles. Now there was only one left and Mr. Cannon was eyeing it.

"What's your son's name?" she asked.

"Kix."

"What's his real name?"

"Kix."

"Poor guy." She shook her head sadly. "He has no chance."

"His mother was a country music fan. I'm told there's a connection," I said. "And also, shut up."

"You're from LA, right?" Mr. Cannon asked. He already knew the answer. He showed up to ask me personal questions every few days.

"Yup."

"What are you doing out here in the country?" Ms. Friedmond asked.

"I wanted to move home," I said. "And I decided I wanted to teach at the last minute. The small, lovely town of South Hill was the closest place that would hire me at the last minute."

"Where's home?"

"Roanoke. Three hours west of here."

"You like the country?" she asked.

"Parts of it."

"South Hill's a real nice place," Mr. Cannon said. "What's not to like?"

"All the personal questions."

"Do you like teaching?" Kristen asked.

"A whole lot."

"Why?"

"Teaching is the greatest act of optimism."

Blank faces. I wondered if teachers read anymore.

"What?" she asked.

"Before I was a youth pastor, I worked in a job that was turning me into a cynic and a pessimist. I dealt with the failings of humanity. But teaching, on the other hand, is about potential and growth. Its focus is the future, not the past."

"Think you'll do it forever?" Ms. Friedmond asked.

"No idea."

"Mr. August, when are you coming over for dinner?" Kristen asked. "You can talk sports with my husband and our kids can punch each other."

"You're wasting your time," Cannon said. "I keep asking him and he's always busy."

Taylor walked in, heels clicking. Her slingbacks were black, her ankles were great, her red skirt was tiny, her button-up black shirt was tight and open at the neck, her earrings were red hoops and she pointedly did not look at me. Her outfits recently were designed to kill, and I could imagine neither her male students being able to pay attention nor Principal Martin remaining silent much longer. I'd been avoiding looking at her for the past two weeks, else I thought of nothing else for the rest of the day. She smiled generally to the room and poured herself a cup of coffee.

"Ms. Williams," Ms. Friedmond laughed. "Come on. I think I just saw your ass."

Taylor turned around, cocked an eyebrow at me and said, "At least someone noticed."

She walked out of the room to the startled, openmouthed laughter from the girls. My heart was beating a little faster.

A young, short, fairly handsome teacher walked in, looking over his shoulder. He looked at us, whistled, and said, "Damn. Think there's room enough for me in that skirt?"

"Not once she fits Mr. August in," Ms. Friedmond said.

"Competition." He grinned. He was my age, fit, wearing the usual khakis and earth-toned button-up. "Last year she used to hit on me. Not this year. This year you showed up."

"She used to hit on you? So *that's* why Roy hates you," Ms. Friedmond murmured. I didn't know Roy yet. So. Many. Teachers.

"Exactly," he said, and offered me his hand. "I'm the other Mackenzie. Mackenzie Allen. I teach band."

"Two Mackenzies," I mused, shaking his hand.

"How'd we get so lucky?" Ms. Friedmond said.

-Ten days until the first body is discovered-

Life was good. No one shot at me. No one looked to me for answers I still searched for myself. I had a set schedule. My coworkers liked me and I liked them. Old scars were healing. I was good at my job, according to preliminary findings by my peers and boss. My housing situation was a dream. Nightmares were receding. I whistled as I drove to work.

The friendly, efficient secretaries smiled at me in the mornings. Students came to visit me during homeroom and talk sports or girls. Kristen and I swapped baby stories, Mackenzie and I swapped fantasy football emails, and Taylor and I made eyes at each other over lunch. During planning periods I fell into an easy routine of working on future lessons, grading papers, eating cafeteria tater-tots, and playing on my computer. After school we hit the fairways and greens, and when we didn't we took mulligans. Kix and I grilled out, took walks and had picnics for dinner. I started losing track of pleasant mornings, fulfilling work, conversations that revolved around life rather than death, sending students to stand outside when they couldn't be quiet, and afternoons in the sun. The weeks stretched out in front of me with no end, and I was content.

The nights were harder. Life and culture had flowed outside of my LA apartment during every hour of the day. Instant access to anything and everything. Now I had to drive fifteen minutes before I saw the first streetlight. My neighborhood was mostly empty because the homeowners only vacationed here during the summer and weekends. I liked some of the people I worked with but didn't live near any of them. And my son had to be in bed by eight every night.

Nothing could go wrong at a peaceful place like this.

So I sat and read and listened to music and watched TV. And thought. And tried not to be lonely. Tonight I took a shower, jumped into bed with a Patrick O'Brien book, and tried not to think about Taylor. One night at a time.

-One day until the body is discovered-

Teachers hate copy machines.

I was a teacher. I hated copiers. South Hill Middle had two copiers, both bought used. Very rarely were both operational. I knew both repairmen by their first names.

"So, Mr. August," Mr. Charlie said. He was the art teacher and substitute pastor, and he was making copies. I was waiting on him. He seemed oblivious, but I liked him anyway. "What do you think about the turmoil on our school board?"

"We have a school board?"

Mackenzie Allen, the band teacher, laughed. I'm so funny. He was flipping through a notebook full of music. With three of us in the workroom, I felt a little bit claustrophobic. What on earth does an art teacher need copies for, anyway?

"You don't read the local paper, August?" Mackenzie Allen asked.

"We have a local paper?"

"You just moved here." Mr. Charlie smiled. He had a nice, slow, significant way of speaking. "I forgot that about you."

"Our school board is on crack," Mackenzie Allen said. "The whole lot of them." He was drinking coffee. I wanted coffee.

"He means the school board don't get along," Mr. Charlie smiled again. He was a smiler. I wanted coffee.

"They hate each other. They hate the Superintendent. They hate the board of supervisors. They hate us. We hate them. It's all one big hate parade."

"Sounds terrific. Where do I sign up?" I said.

"It's not Christian to hate," Mr. Charlie said.

"You're funny, Mr. August. Mack. I like you, Mack. You're all right," Mackenzie Allen said. I wished he had a different name.

"I just try to stay out of it," Mr. Charlie said.

"He's right, Mr. August. Mr. Charlie's right. Just stay the heck away. Steer clear. Don't get in the middle."

"Stay out of it," I repeated slowly. "Think I can remember that."

The door opened and another man walked in. A tall, strong black man. A tall, strong black man who looked about 55 and had a stunning white beard and stunning white teeth when he smiled.

"Hey, Mr. Suhr," Mackenzie Allen said. There were four men in the room and no women. What were the odds? Not good, in a school that had four times as many women employees as men.

"Hello, sirs," the enormous happy man said, smile flashing. His voice filled the room. "So nice to see you. I hope you're well today." He stopped and looked at me for a moment. Then smiled. "My, you're a big fellow."

"Isn't that the pot calling the kettle...well, you know," I said, and he laughed. Threw back his head and laughed. We shook hands.

"I'm Mr. Suhr. I teach shop and robotics. You're Mr. August, aren't you?" He was still shaking my hand.

"That's me," I said.

"The Lord is with you, Mr. August," he said. He still had my hand, only now he was holding it with both hands. Oddly enough, I didn't feel uncomfortable.

"And also with you," I repeated from memory from years sitting in a pew.

Christians. Everywhere.

"No, no," he said, and shook his finger at me. Then he placed that hand on my shoulder. "I mean that the Lord, Mr. August, is with you. When I heard about you from Mr. Charlie, my heart leaped within me."

I didn't know what to say, so I went with that. Mr. Charlie had apparently been talking about me.

"I am glad you are here."

"Thank you, Mr. Suhr," I said. "Glad to be here."

"Good," he said, and released me. "Good. Please come visit me in the shop one day soon, and we will talk."

"Happy to."

"Good," he said again. He fed change into the drink machine, bought a diet soda, and said to us, "Peace be with you." Then he left.

"I didn't know the Lord was with you, August," Mackenzie Allen said.

"Yeah, but I don't like to brag."

Mr. Charlie frowned at me.

11

Early morning, but not chilly. Apparently the temperature doesn't drop until winter in South Hill. I pulled into work earlier than usual to make copies. It was the simple things in life that made me smile. But not this morning.

I saw a body lying in the trailer quad on my way to get the papers. A dead body. Corpses are easy to distinguish from the unconscious with just a little experience, which I had. Not unconscious. Dead. Male, facedown, dressed like a teacher. Students would be arriving in forty-five minutes.

I took out my cell as I crouched beside the body. No pulse. Dew on the skin.

"911. What's your emergency?"

"This is Mack August calling from South Hill Middle School. There is a corpse, white male, about 20 feet from the inner south entrance to the school."

"Can you verify the man is dead?" the female voice asked.

"Yes. No pulse. I haven't searched for identification. I'll be here when the cavalry arrives."

I hung up and did my best to remember that I was a teacher now. I didn't look at the body.

The dispatcher probably contacted the sheriff's office immediately, but first on the scene was the school's resource officer. Gun drawn. I managed to not roll my eyes.

Resource officers are local law enforcement agents assigned to schools. Their lives can be pretty uneventful besides breaking up the occasional fight and finding drugs in lockers. The RO at our school was named Steve, and he'd obviously been put at the school to keep him out of the sheriff's hair and office. He compensated for being overweight and low man on the totem pole by acting tough, though he would never have made it through a larger city's academy.

"Don't move," he called, walking in from the parking lot, gun gripped in both fists, moving sideways in a crablike motion.

"Sure thing," I said. I was sitting several feet away on the sidewalk, arms around my knees.

"Keep your hands where I can see them!"

"I'll try," I assured him.

Steve was uncertain what he should do, so he alternated between staring at the body and looking around corners suspiciously.

"Just the two of us. You can holster your piece," I said.

"Quiet," he barked at me. I hoped whoever arrived next would have some experience with a crime scene. A pair of handcuffs clattered to the ground next to me. "Put those on."

I looked down at them. I was pretty sure he wasn't making a joke, and I almost felt bad for him. I tossed them back. They landed at his feet.

"No. Put your gun away."

"What?" he yelled at me. He was wired, lots of adrenaline, puffed up with importance. Wasn't going to take much to set him off. "You're under arrest."

"You can't cuff me for coming to work and finding a body. You *can* cuff me, however, for what I'll do to you if you try."

The barrel of his gun dropped a few inches as he stared at me in disbelief. His face began to turn red in anger.

"Oh jeez," I sighed and stood. "Listen, I'm sorry. I know you're trying. But you are not going to cuff me. I work here, I found the body,

I called 911, I'm not going anywhere. And put your gun away. He's been dead a while, and maybe from natural causes. If not, bad guys are way gone. I'll go see if Principal Martin is in her office. You stay here and...make sure the body isn't stolen."

I walked off and left him speechless. I knew neither of the principals had come into work yet. The resource officer needed a favor so I decided to leave and let him realize he didn't know what he was doing without an audience. I went in the hallway and helped the wall stay standing by leaning on it.

Cool, emotionless mechanics had taken over when I saw the body. I did everything right and didn't feel. Now, though, I began to feel things. I felt the sick dread in my stomach as old emotions surfaced. Somewhere, peripherally, I felt sad because I thought I knew the guy. Mostly though, I tried to fight off memories.

Red and blue lights began flickering on the hallway walls. Still, I waited. Officers walked by the doorway, calm voices, radios squawking. I waited some more and then walked outside. Two unmarked squad cars and three law enforcement agents had arrived.

A deputy sheriff wearing a badge with the name "Andrews" also wore latex gloves and was crouched beside the corpse, going softly through pockets. Andrews was all-American good-looking. Probably used to be a good baseball player. A second deputy was snapping digital pictures. They both wore the flat-brimmed Stetsons I'd always secretly wanted to try on.

"That's him."

The RO was standing beside a man who had to be the sheriff. He appeared to be forty-five, had a marine-style haircut, looked like he lifted weights every day and went jogging every few, and wore a crisp beige and brown uniform with the star on the chest. He was taking notes on a clip board. Good sign. Principal Martin was also there, wide-eyed with her hand over her mouth. She looked at me and so did the sheriff.

"You found the body?" the sheriff asked me. His voice was soft but firm.

"Twenty minutes ago." I nodded. "Checked for a pulse and let him lie."

"Good man," he said and pointed at the corpse. "ID him?"

"Didn't try. Got an educated guess."

"The coroner should be arriving soon. No need for guesses."

"That's convenient," Ms. Martin murmured. Her eyes were wet, staring into space.

"Pardon, ma'am?" he asked.

"Mr. August found the body," she said.

"Why is that convenient?"

"He used to be a police officer."

12

S quad cars kept rolling in, including one South Hill Police cruiser. South Hill had a small five man police force, in addition to the county sheriff's department located in Boydton, ten miles away. The Sheriff, Sheriff Chandler Mitchell, stood by and took notes, but Detective Andrews ran the show. The crime scene was taped off and the investigation shifted to a close inspection of the sidewalk and grass surrounding the body. So far, the investigation seemed pretty small-time, but then again it was a small town. I had grown accustomed to a circus.

I made a statement, promised to be available, and got out of the way. I left to make copies as the coroner arrived. Soon the body would be rolled over and most of the questions would be answered.

Concentrating was hard with the investigation happening directly outside of my window, but I stayed in my trailer and gave it a shot.

I was pretty sure I knew the victim. He was young, about my age, and in good health. Odds were in favor of foul play over heart attack.

Buses began rolling in ten minutes short of eight. They usually lined up one after the other, until the bell rang at the top of the hour, and the students would come pouring out of the folding yellow doors. Today eight passed without a bell. I shook my head, glad I wasn't a bus driver this morning.

Sending six hundred middle school kids home isn't easy. When it's an issue of snow, everyone knows it's a possibility and is semi-prepared for it. But when hundreds of parents aren't home and aren't expecting kids to be home for eight hours, the situation gets sticky. I shook my head, glad I wasn't a principal.

The intercom beeped three times and a voice asked all teachers to report to the cafeteria. I obeyed. The crime scene was directly between my trailer door and the school's door, so I walked around it. The body had been rolled over and I could see his face. My guess was right. Sheriff Mitchell was on a cell, probably trying to find the line between a thorough investigation and a quick one. I shook my head, glad I wasn't the sheriff. The second wave of buses was pulling in and having a hard time finding places to park. The assistant principal was running between bus doors. I walked inside to find the PE teachers herding car-driven kids into the gym. Sleepiness was working on the side of the teachers; the teenagers were willing to be quietly herded, looking anxious, rather than excited, about the change in routine. They sat quietly on the bleachers talking as I passed.

Mr. Cannon met me in the hall, pointed over his shoulder with his thumb toward the crime scene, and said, "Real shame, isn't it."

"Sure is."

"You had just met him, right?"

"Yup. About two weeks ago."

"Real shame." He shook his head.

Most of the staff was already waiting in the cafeteria. Taylor beckoned me over to sit near her.

"Is it true?" she whispered. Her question was loud enough to draw the attention of our neighbors.

"Depends on what you heard."

"Somebody had a heart attack."

"Dunno," I said.

"Yes you do. I heard you found the body."

"I did," I said. "But you shouldn't listen to gossip."

"So you found the body," she frowned at me, "but you don't know if they're dead?"

"Definitely dead. Police haven't issued an official ID yet, though. Nor the cause of death. And by the way, it's 'if *he or she* is dead.'"

She glared at my correction and said, "But you know, though."

"Just guesses."

"Tell me."

"Gossip, gossip." I shook a finger at her. She did not think that was cute, but experience had taught me to keep my mouth shut.

"I also heard you were a homicide detective," she said, and nudged me with her shoulder. I didn't respond, even though she had a very nice shoulder. "Ms. Martin didn't show us that part of your resume."

I shrugged.

"So, are you a detective?"

"Not currently, no."

"Stop, you know what I mean. Were you? I mean, I knew you were a cop, but not a homicide detective," she said.

"A lot of officers don't like the term 'cop,' you know."

"Does it bother you?"

"Newp," I said.

"Okay then. Were you?"

"Yup."

"Shut up, in LA?"

I shushed her as Principal Martin walked to the front of the cafeteria benches. I was glad to get out of that interrogation. Uninvited personal question and answer sessions made me grouchy.

"Hi everybody, thanks for being so patient," she said. Her eyes were red. "As you may have heard, a dead body was discovered out near the south trailers this morning by Mr. August. It appears to be a man, and we're guessing the man probably works here. Worked here."

Heads began to swivel around, looking for missing faces. Not mine.

"The police are doing their best to figure out what happened, and when I know more I'll let you know."

She said police, but she meant the sheriff's office or law enforcement agents, something like that. Somewhere along the way, 'police' had become the umbrella term to cover everything related to law enforcement. It's the little things in life that annoy me.

"We're not sure yet what we're doing about the students. There are six hundred kids waiting out in the buses, but obviously a portion of the campus is a crime scene and might stay that way for a while."

She went on to talk about precedents and procedures, but Taylor nudged me again.

"Is that why you're so big?" she whispered.

"What?"

"Because of the cop thing?"

"Sorta. I did some pushups last week too."

"Okay." She rolled her eyes, but she liked me. "Why didn't you tell me you had a kid?"

"Don't you have a kid?"

"Hell no," her voice squeaked.

I shrugged and said, "I thought everyone did."

A guy across the table shushed us. His name was Roy. He was the agriculture teacher. He hated everyone named Mackenzie in the school. Especially if Taylor hit on them. I felt his name was very appropriate for his appearance, and he obviously had a thing for Taylor. Most of the guys in the school did. Glancing around, I saw we were surrounded by guys. The entire cafeteria was women, except for the circle around her. I was going to sit somewhere else next time.

The vice principal walked through the doors with the sheriff, and the three of them had a two-minute huddle. I went to the back of the cafeteria, pretending to throw something away. The room buzzed with whispers until Principal Martin addressed them again. She did not look well. She was a tough lady, but unexpected death is unnerving, even to those used to it.

"The body has been identified. He has no immediate family, and the police are contacting his parents. So we can tell you that it is Mackenzie Allen."

Gasps and sobs around the room. I had only just met him recently. I liked him. Great guy. Hard to picture him involved in stuff worth killing over.

"We can't send the kids home so we've got to finish out the day as best we can, and we'll probably announce later that there will be no school tomorrow. Obviously we'll get a sub for Mr. Allen's class. Mr. August, Ms. Williams and Ms. Friedmond, you'll need to have class in the cafeteria today."

The meeting broke so we could go shepherd students to the proper places. Taylor met me and started cursing about what a nightmare having class in the cafeteria would be. I was about to agree with her when I stopped and realized it could be a lot worse. I was glad I wasn't Mackenzie Allen.

13

School finally let out after a long day of shouting and echoes in the cafeteria. News crews filmed the buses rolling away as reporters with microphones spoke with somber, serious tones in the foreground. I'd cancelled golf practice, which meant I had a couple hours to spare before I was scheduled to pick up Kix. Which meant I went to Applebees for a drink.

I hadn't scouted out local bars yet. I felt like a sissy going to an Applebees restaurant for a beer, but I was hoping no one would notice. Instead, Detective Andrews tracked me down. Drat. Busted.

He ordered a beer and joined me at my back table. He had great hair.

"Want another one?" he asked. "I'm buying."

"Thanks. No."

"Sure?" he asked.

"Sure."

"You're a better man than I am."

"You noticed," I said.

He chuckled and took a drink. I knew what was coming.

"Sheriff wants to know if you have an alibi."

"Don't need one."

"Hell, I know," he said. "But it'll give me some defense."

"For talking with me," I said. He was in an unusual position. The initial discoverer of the body is always a remote candidate for a suspect. Rarely does that person turn out to be the culprit, but it happens. If I had an alibi then a frank discussion would be less questionable. And he wanted to have a discussion because of my previous job. And probably because of my fantastic sense of humor.

"Right on."

"I have a weak one," I said. "I'm raising a nine-month-old baby alone. If I killed him, I either have a babysitter or I'm hauling around a baby on my back the whole night."

"Pretty weak."

"Yup," I agreed.

"I called LA."

"Figured you would," I said.

"Talked to Captain Jeffrey."

"Lucky you."

"Sweet guy."

"Sweet as motor oil," I agreed, and took a drink.

"Said LAPD got you from Highway Patrol, which got you from college, mad at the world and out to kill yourself. He also said you were promoted to detective faster than anyone he's had in ten years. That you got an unreal nose for the bad guy."

"You should see me in my Spider-Man hero tights," I said.

"You worked some high-profile cases, including the North murders, got your name in the papers. Then you quit after two years," he said, glancing down at his notepad. I said nothing. "And now you're involved in a murder investigation in my county."

"I'm not involved."

"Still mad at the world?"

"Not anymore," I said. "He tell you what I did after I left?"

"He did. Church gig."

"If I could still be doing that, I would. I'm just awful at it."

"Finding the body shake you up?"

"Don't think so. Tonight might be a different story."

"What made you leave homicide?" he asked.

"I was seduced by the teacher salary."

"Fine, don't tell me."

"Okay," I said.

"I'm not asking for anything," he said, growing a little irritated with me. "But there is a murder investigation going on in your school."

"You saw that too, huh?"

"And you happen to have experience with homicide. If alarms start going off in your head, I wanna know about it. That's all."

"Sheriff know you're talking to me?"

"The sheriff..." He paused and searched for the right phrasing. "The sheriff is confident his department will handle this no problem. I'm more willing to accept help, I suppose. Especially from a pro."

"Small caliber gunshot to the forehead. No exit hole. Powder burn on the skin. Body was moved posthumously. Anything else obvious that I'm missing?"

"Looks like he drove himself to the school," he said.

"Hm."

"Hm," he agreed.

"I hear alarms, you'll know."

14

I lived ten miles off Interstate 85, deep into tobacco country. The lake was worth the drive, and so were the stars. I sat on the dock behind my rented house drinking a beer. My Ugly Stick fishing rod was out, and I hoped a catfish would bite the bobbing liver bait, but it wasn't the right time of night. I just wanted something to do. The night air felt warm, my canvas chair creaked anytime I shifted, a citronella torch burned to keep away bugs, my beer was cold, and the baby monitor hissed softly on the dock beside me. Life was good. Other than Mackenzie Allen still being dead.

A car pulled into my driveway, parked, and went quiet. I assumed a followup visit on the investigation, so I didn't get up. I was tired of the questions for one day. The headlights turned off and I could hear someone walking down to join me.

I was wrong. Mr. Charlie, the art teacher and substitute pastor, stepped into the torch light and nodded to me.

"Howdy," I said.

"Good evening, Mr. August. May I sit down?" he asked and unfolded my other chair. I slid the cooler over to him. He took a bottle without saying anything. I didn't know Mr. Charlie that well, but I was glad for company. He didn't seem to be in the mood to talk yet, so we sat staring at the stars and water. Eventually I regretted sliding the cooler over. There was one beer left. Mr. Charlie hadn't opened his yet. I'd just finished my second. After scanning my options for subtly getting the cooler back, I set the bottle down dramatically on the side of my chair closest to him, hoping for a positive reaction. "Him and I were close," he said, and twisted off the cap.

"Mackenzie Allen?"

"Yes," he said.

"How close?"

"Not like brothers. Went to my churches some," he said. "Like, good friends."

Another long silence. His drink was half gone. I started to get nervous. However, I had the good friend of a murder victim on the verge of rambling. Useful information often surfaced during rambles.

"I just met him," I said. "Seemed like a great guy."

"Yes," he said. "He was, he was. It's got me spooked, Mr. August."

"Spooked?"

"Yessir, spooked. Worried, you know, wondering what all happened." His voice was slow and calm, but also haunted.

"Me too. Doesn't seem like the type who'd be involved in the stuff that gets one shot."

"He wasn't," he said. "No sir."

"Did he work on the side?"

"What do you mean?" he asked.

"You know, own his own lawn care company? Bartend? Deliver papers?"

"No."

"Was he into drugs?"

"No," he said.

"Not even pot?"

"Well, Mr. August," he said slowly. "I don't wish to disrespect the dead. But he'd smoke some dope once a while. I told him his body was a temple, but he never listened. His guy is an old friend of ours."

"His dealer?"

"Yes."

"Pot isn't usually worth killing over," I said. "Doesn't cost enough. What was he doing at the school so late?"

"I wish I knew, Mr. August."

"Dating anyone?" I asked.

"No, his girlfriend moved a long time ago. He was single since then."

"Gambling?"

"Just Friday night poker once a month. Twenty dollar buy-in."

"High roller."

"Yessir." He grinned.

"Sounds squeaky to me."

"Squeaky clean," he agreed.

"Which is why you're spooked."

"Yes," he agreed again. He picked up the last bottle and opened it. Shucks. "So are you going to catch them?"

"Catch?"

"I hear you some kind of super cop."

"Nah," I said. Someone had been talking. And exaggerating. Double shucks. "Used to be a regular cop. That's it."

"A regular cop?"

"Just an ordinary, regular cop."

"Not a detective?" he asked.

"Just an ordinary, regular detective. Not even a private detective."

"So, are you going to catch the perpetrator?"

"Yup."

15

A hazy morning, and a few camera crews were set up just outside the school lawn. I made it to my trailer without finding any dead bodies, which is how I preferred my pre-school routine. I carried a wrapped plate of biscuits smothered in sausage gravy. At least half of my mornings would have been spent hungry without Leta's generosity.

No school yesterday. Kix and I had spent a lazy day at home. We practiced crawling and saw no improvement, and he practiced Halo, even though he just turned in circles, fired at the ground, and got whooped by the Brutes. I'd also gotten in a jog, pushing Kix around the neighborhood in his jogging stroller.

The murder had made the six o'clock news in Richmond. Few details were given because few details were known. The reporter said that a fellow teacher had discovered the body. I'm famous.

My conversation with Mr. Charlie had not given me anything to report to the police. Other than pot, which might show in the autopsy, but probably wasn't a lead. I mused over my quick response that I'd find whoever killed Mackenzie Allen. The sheriff or the police would probably catch the killer. They usually did. If they didn't, I was going to try. For two reasons. One, I was good at it. Two, I had liked Mackenzie. But I'd give the law a day or two.

My key hung from a blue and gold school lanyard around my neck. I pulled it over my head, unlocked my door and pushed in. Steam rose from my breakfast when I unwrapped it. I popped the top of a Diet Pepsi and attempted to enjoy the last ten minutes before eight a.m.

Five of the minutes went by before I noticed a note card resting on my keyboard. The paper was white, and letters cut from a magazine had been pasted onto it. It read, "**BE CAREFUL WITH WHOM YOU'RE FRIENDS.**"

16

My classes were bleak, understandably so. Many students were still processing the death. Some kids had gone home, had no one to talk to because their single parent worked, and were now back at school ready to vent. Guidance counselors were in and out of the room, pulling out students who didn't seem to be coping very well.

During my planning period I retrieved an old fingerprint kit from the trunk of my Accord. Not a very tough car, but it had never broken down and was great on gas. Plus, I love Hondas. Other oddities in my trunk: handcuffs, belt holster, and a baseball bat.

No fingerprints surfaced on the card. I also dusted the backrest on my chair, in case the note-placer had pulled it backwards. I got a few big prints and lifted them, even though I figured they were mine.

I probably shouldn't assume the note was related to the murder. Nor should I assume the note was from the killer. But I was doing both. If that was true, the dynamic of the crime shifted dramatically.

If the note was from Mackenzie Allen's killer, it suggested the murderer, on some level, wanted to be caught. If not caught then at least discovered. Like a child showing off a finger painting to a parent, or a disruptive student enjoying the notoriety from the class and attention from the teacher, the goal is recognition, significance, and possibly approval. The mental awareness of the consequences of being caught is dominated by the human desire to be noticed and appreciated. The consequences for murder are severe enough to indicate extreme imbalance in the person ignoring them to chase attention.

I think.

If I was the only recipient of a note, then I was intended to be the catcher or discoverer. My attention was being sought. My approval was worth killing for. For reasons unknown to me, I was very compelling to the killer.

Not something I wanted to be.

If the note was from the killer. And that was a big if. I'd been involved in similar cases, but only as the investigator and not the object of the obsession. I wasn't sure if I was evaluating the situation rationally yet. I had been in South Hill for just a few weeks. Didn't seem long enough to foster an obsession. Nor was I a celebrity, powerful, or even that interesting.

How did the note-leaver gain entrance into my room? Did they have a key? I saw no signs of forced entry. No window screens were ripped. Initial guesses pointed to an individual with access to a key. Did the teacher who occupied the trailer last year still have a copy? Custodians, administrators, secretaries? Anyone standing close enough to the box where extra keys were kept? Anybody with even slight talent at picking locks?

I kicked around theories in my head all day, prompting Mr. Charlie, Kristen Short, Mrs. Ballard, and Mr. Cannon to ask me at different times if I was doing okay. Evidently I looked shocked. And considering I discovered the body it was no wonder, Mrs. Ballard told me.

I locked my door after eighth period, though apparently getting past the lock wasn't much of a challenge. The day had been long and trying. Hitting golf balls at the Country Club sounded about right.

"Hey, city boy," the resource officer said. He was leaning on the brick wall beside the sidewalk. His thumbs were tucked behind his belt, which was too tight. He had dip behind his lip.

"Hey, Barney Fife," I said in return. My conscience twitched and I stopped. "No, listen, I apologize. I gave you a hard time the other day and I shouldn't have."

"You apologize?" he said. He spit on the sidewalk near my foot. "Fuck your apology. You big stuff out in California. But out here, in the good 'ol Commonwealth of Virginia, you listen to me. I'm the law and you ain't."

"You spell 'Commonwealth' and I'll give you five bucks."

"Next time I tell you to do something," he said as he shoved off the wall to approach me, "like put handcuffs on, you better listen. Cause, city boy, I don't play nice."

"This is a great speech," I said. He stopped just inches from me. I wasn't fazed by his intimidation tactic. He wouldn't try anything on school grounds. And if he did, I could take him while grading papers. "You should try it out on the killer. How's that going, by the way? Found 'em yet? Too busy practicing tough?"

"Don'choo worry about the killer," he said softly. "Sum'bitch like you, better watch out for yourself."

I sniffed. Behind the cheap cologne and underneath the tobacco was the faint smell of marijuana. I glanced at his eyes for confirmation. The RO was high.

17

At the golf course I forewent the traditional teaching on the driving range. Today felt like a good day to simply golf. There was no back nine, so we divided up into two foursomes and teed off. I was in the second group and waiting for my turn when Detective Andrews stepped up beside me. The wind didn't ruffle his all-American hair.

"Beautiful day," I said.

"Have a minute?"

"You fellas go ahead," I told the group of three middle school gents, staring openly at us. "I have to teach the Deputy how to hot-wire a car. I'll catch up."

"I never learned how to do that," he said as we walked to the side of the clubhouse.

"I did. Never used it though. I should rustle up an old-fashioned car chase."

"The victim is coming up clean," he said. "Cell phone records, credit card, townhouse is clean, car is clean, everyone we've talked to waxes about what a nice, normal guy he was."

"Squeaky."

"Slug is a .22, handgun, close range."

"Found the location of original shooting?" I asked.

"Negative. Nothing shows on school surveillance either. And a standard Kleenex was used to clean the victim's face."

"Face was cleaned?"

"Yes," he answered.

"Weird."

"Agreed. Any alarms?" he asked.

Sure. He smoked pot. So does the officer at the school where he worked. The same officer who told me not to worry about the killer. And someone left me a note telling me to be careful with my friend selection.

"A .22," I said.

"So?"

"You never seen the movies? Tough-guy killers carry bigger guns than that."

"That's all you got, huh?"

"The gun is most likely silenced, because even a little .22 would wake the neighbors, but the lack of shells means he is either picking them up or using a revolver. Finding a .22 revolver that will fit a silencer is difficult, so this guy is probably careful."

"Can't figure a girl," he said.

"Unless she's a hoss. Or had help carrying the body." We stood silent for a moment, watching the golfers tee off. "Small handgun, close range, victim still in work clothes, no sign of struggle at his place, probably drove himself to school, body moved, face cleaned."

"Right on."

"I don't get it," I said.

"Agreed."

ALL OF THE golfers left except for Stephen. He stood by the putting green, hitting the tips of his shoes with his pitching wedge. I dropped a few practice balls nearby, and chipped one onto the green.

"Your mom coming, Stephen?"

"I hope so."

"Hope so?"

"Sometimes she forgets," he mumbled.

"What about your dad?"

"He died last year. Cancer."

"I'm sorry, Stephen. I didn't know."

He shrugged and started stepping onto his golf balls hard enough to press them halfway into the earth.

"Your mom just getting off work?"

"No. After she drops me off at home, she goes to work the night shift."

"You stay home alone?"

"My sister is in tenth grade."

Unfortunately, his story wasn't very rare. I'd deduced from random comments that several of my students put themselves to bed while their parents were out working, drinking, or playing bingo.

"Something else bothering you?"

He shrugged again, and started kicking at the half-buried balls. I looked around to make sure none of the groundskeepers were watching.

"You take band, don't you?"

He nodded.

"All three years?"

He nodded again.

"So you were close with Mr. Allen, the teacher who died."

"He came to my dad's funeral."

"Mr. Allen sounds like he was a great guy. I wish I'd gotten to know him better."

Stephen nodded. I stood there with my arms crossed, holding my putter, watching Stephen kicking halfheartedly at golf balls, and felt like an idiot. Did I have no encouragement? No support to offer? I felt like I should, but nothing came out of my mouth.

I stood frozen until his mom pulled up and honked her horn. Stephen grabbed his clubs.

"See ya, Mr. August," he said before slamming the door behind him.

"I'm a jerk," I said as they drove away.

18

M y face was hot and sensitive after the round. It always was. I turned the car on, threw my sweaty hat in the back and drove off toward Leta's house to pick up Kix. My favorite part of the day. By far.

Either the sheriff or Detective Andrews was holding out on me. Toxicology would certainly have come back by now and probably revealed marijuana use, but Andrews didn't share that with me.

I punched a number in my phone and got an answer on the third ring.

"Sergeant Bingham," the voice said.

"August," I replied, identifying myself.

"You don't say." The voice on the other end belonged to my old sergeant. He had been primarily responsible for pulling me into the homicide division. He was a hard-nosed, gritty boss who hated murderers and loved the men and women who worked for him.

"Fraid so," I said.

"It's a good thing I was sitting down. Might have fallen over backwards, on accounta how full of joy I suddenly am."

"I knew it."

"You coming back here?" he asked. I could hear him chewing on a tooth-pick around his words.

"Negative."

"Then get off my damn phone," he said.

"I need a favor."

"What."

"I'm quasi-involved in a murder investigation down here," I said.

"I heard. Captain got a call from...somebody. People get murdered in Virginia?"

"Yup."

"That's a shame," he said.

"If I overnight something to you, can you run the prints? I think they're mine but I want to check."

The line was silent for a few seconds.

"I thought you were consulting. How involved are you?"

"Got more involved today. I think I received a note from the killer."

"You would," he sighed.

"Prints?"

"Virginia can't run prints?"

"Mostly we churn butter and fight off the British," I said.

"And?"

"And," I said, "I don't want word to leak that I got a note. Which it would, if I handle it locally. Might scare him off. Or her."

"You wish, her."

I grinned. "A little bit."

"Send them through. Hey," he said.

"Yeah."

"We have too many people here right now. Might have to transfer a couple out. But your job is waiting for you as soon as you want it."

"Thanks. Means a lot."

"Miss it?" he asked.

"A little. No one shoots at me here though."

"Give them time. They just met you."

19

"FANBOYS," I said. My students looked at me expectantly, pens poised, eager to learn. At least one of them did. "That's how you can remember conjunctions. For, and, nor, but, or, yet, and so. On your test, remember Fanboys."

"Mr. August," Jon said and raised his hand. Jumping Jon the golfer. "Did you make that up?"

"Of course I did. That's what I do in my spare time. Think of mnemonics for you."

"Do you really?"

"No. However," I said, but the door opened. Ms. Friedmond, the sassy science teacher, walked in and approached my podium. She was supposed to raise her hand before approaching the podium, but I decided I wouldn't give her silent lunch.

"Mackenzie Allen's funeral is Friday," she said softly. "We just found out. The school is letting out at noon that day."

"Ms. Friedmond, you don't belong in here," one of the students informed her.

She turned around and said, "Your momma."

The students laughed.

"Can we say that to students?" I whispered.

"Your momma too," she told me.

"She's no longer with us," I said. Dramatically. That should show her.

"Then all her sisters." She cocked an eyebrow at me. "Tell your students about Friday." Then she walked out, waving Miss America style to the class. I liked her as much as all the students did. Which is a lot.

THE FUNERAL WAS HELD at First Baptist Church, near the bed and breakfast in which I was once visited by Taylor. The school closed early so students and teachers could go. I was surprised by the turnout. Over three hundred people, I'd guess. Cousins and uncles of the victim greeted at the door. Mackenzie Allen's mother was a widow and she sat in the front, and I could hear sobbing from the back row. Up until now I hadn't thought much about his family and their nearly unbearable grief. The mystery, the confusion, the ongoing investigation only added to the pain. My heart began to ache from the weeping.

But I didn't stay long.

Mackenzie's townhouse was three miles from the church, halfway to the middle school. I got there in five minutes. As I drove, I considered the odds of the murderer being at the funeral. Pretty good, I'd bet. All signs were pointing to him being murdered by someone he knew.

His back door was cheap sliding glass. With a little rocking, the latch lifted free and the door slid open. The two-story townhouse smelled the way all vacated victims' homes do. Empty, lifeless, and the hint of fingerprint powder.

I wasn't sure what I was looking for. I hoped I would know it when I saw it. An alarm might go off, who knew.

He was a neat guy, with all his band teacher paraphernalia fastidiously stacked around the room. It looked like he might have played three different wind instruments plus guitar and piano. Small TV, no video games, laptop computer, digital camera nicer than mine. Juice and beer in the fridge, soup and canned fruit in the pantry, Oreos on the counter, Bagel Bites in the freezer. KFC bag in the trash.

Spare bedroom had winter clothes in the closet and a set of drums. Lucky neighbors.

I apologized to him for invading his privacy but explained that it might help bring about justice. I hoped he understood and then went into his bedroom.

Family pictures in little frames, spare change and cologne on top of the dresser. Pictures of friends pinned next to his closet. Bed unmade, empty glasses on the nightstand. He was reading *Season of Life*. Lots of shoes and shirts in the closet. No pornography or anything else under the mattress, no secret notes or letters in drawers, nothing unusual in pockets. His bank statement was open on his desk. He made a little more than me. But he also had a car payment, which I did not. Small victories. He made no marks on his wall calendar. I sat down in his desk chair and looked and thought.

The townhouse did not smell like pot. Good sign he was just a casual user, maybe smoked out back.

I left after fifty-five minutes, knowing nothing more than when I entered.

20

M y phone rang as I drove away from the townhouse.

"August," I said.

"Bingham," he replied.

"Yo."

"The prints off the chair are yours," he said on speakerphone.

"Shucks."

"Shucks?"

"It's what we say in Virginia," I said.

"In California we just cuss."

"So do the eighth graders in my class," I said.

"Are you saying LAPD has the vocabulary of thirteen-year-olds?"

"If the shoe fits. What about that card?"

"Nothing special. Standard note card, you can get them at any store, letters came from *People* magazine or equivalent, and glue stick adhesive. No prints."

"Shucks," I said again.

"You remember everything you need to about getting a note from the killer? That's some heavy stuff."

"Think so."

"Pretty hairy, August. Get yourself some backup."

"I might let the local fuzz in on it," I said.

"Do it."

"Yes sir, Sergeant Bingham, sir."

"Hang in there," he said.

"This too shall pass."

21

"So basically," Curtis said, "all the other teachers had over two weeks to prepare for students. You had two days."

"Basically," I answered.

Curtis Shortt was Kristen Shortt's husband. They'd hooked me up with Kix's babysitter. He had a degree in finance and did something in the accounting department at a local corporate office. His slacks were pressed, his blue shirt had a white collar without buttons, his cufflinks were gold and he still wore his tie for dinner. His glasses were rimless. He had the build of a long-distance runner. Kristen was an excellent teacher, or so I gathered by watching her tell kids to slow down in the hallway, and she had excellent taste, or so I gathered from her choice of Leta and James, the babysitters.

The Shortts had just finished building their new home, a modest two-story house with a garage. The walls were brilliant, the wooden floors gleamed, the carpet was fresh, the trim a modern white. They shopped at Ikea. I bet Curtis the finance whiz had decided to build so he could play with prices for everything in the house. We finished dinner. Kix and Jessica were taking turns stealing Elmo books away from each other on the floor.

"Damn. I can't imagine," he said, and took a small, measured sip of wine. Gewurtztramiener. I brought it. Kristen had made soup. "I cannot imagine working with middle school students."

"Let me help," I said. "You work with numbers on the computer, and I work with students in a classroom. So, imagine a tax column on your revenue and expense forms trying to switch places with the column of September's expenses every time you look away from the computer screen, hoping you won't notice."

Kristen laughed and said, "That's pretty good."

"Or you try to print out a summary of payroll and your computer says to you, 'No.' So you hit print again and again, 'No.' Then you call in your boss but the printer refuses to print so your boss takes the computer and printer away and you can get it back tomorrow after it's been in detention."

"Or your mouse grunts and says, 'Mm! That's nice,' and looks at your butt every time you pass," Kristen said. She had dressed up for the dinner, wearing brown slacks, a tight V-necked shirt with an over-sized collar and a thin silver necklace.

"Or the letter 'K' on your keyboard keeps wanting to go see the nurse," I said.

"You're a funny guy, Mack," Curtis said.

I pointed at him with the hand holding my wineglass. "You've obviously been drinking."

Nah. I'm a funny guy. Curtis was correct.

"Before this you were a police officer?"

"Before this I worked at a church. Before that I worked for LAPD."

"Mack-of-all-trades."

"Pun intended." Kristen rolled her eyes. "And before that," she said, "he played football for Radford."

"I think Kristen has a little crush on you," Curtis told me.

"Just a little one." She grinned.

"Don't get too excited," Curtis said. "She crushes easily."

"And you don't get too worried," she replied. "He's a preacher. And a good man."

"A cute, good preacher?" Curtis asked.

"I never said he was cute. Much too scary for my taste. And don't forget football player," she said.

Kix tugged at my pants and held up his hands. I set him in my lap and he began pointing out food on my plate he wanted.

"I'm pretty impressive," I agreed. "Zero for twenty-one as a starter."

"The team was new, right?" Curtis asked.

"Yup. First two years. So we were terrible. Our middle linebacker was an English major."

"A cop with an English degree," Curtis said. "How'd that happen?"

I finished my wine and set the glass down. Kix munched on crust. I had not discussed the specifics of my past with anyone in South Hill. Trying to leave it behind, I suppose. Not letting anyone in, though, was a good way to not make friends. Not making friends was a good way to be lonely.

"I was once engaged. She graduated from Radford and moved north to work. I stayed in Radford to finish my degree that fall. She was shot and killed in the Brooklyn mass shooting soon after arrival and I went nuts. Instead of joining the military I joined the California Highway Patrol. Better pay, got to stay in the States, still got to chase bad guys and shoot guns."

Kristen tilted her head to the side and said with sincerity, "Oh Mack, geez, I'm so sorry."

I was used to it.

"The Brooklyn shooting," Curtis said. "One of those militant Islamic extremism rampages, right?"

"It's been over nine years. I'm no longer dealing with it. Now I'm dealing with the repercussions of dealing with it incorrectly. Nine years from now, I'm hoping I look back on my teaching decision as a good one."

"You said LAPD. That's not the Highway Patrol," Curtis said. He was sharp. I wondered if he'd do my taxes.

"It's easier to get into Highway Patrol. They're desperate, and signed me up on sight. I transferred to LAPD after a year and a half. I'm not cut out to sit in a car."

"So where does Kix fit in?"

"If only we had dessert," I said, "there'd be time for that story."

22

Two in the morning. I was woken by a ruckus outside my house. Several loud thumps against the wall. I sat up straight and almost spilled Kix out of my lap.

It was Friday night, so we'd stayed up late playing games and watching Sesame Street off the Tivo. I'd fallen asleep with a smile on my face as I compared my current contentment to the self-destructive years I spent fashioning my body into a fighting machine, followed by the one year dramatic overcorrection working at a church. Followed by teaching. And peace. My son slept on my chest. The cherry on top.

And now there was a ruckus outside my house. Peace disrupted. This wasn't a dream of gunfire and screaming, echoing in my skull. This was real life.

I stood and walked quickly to the hall closet, Kix in my arms. He stirred, peered at me, and put his head back on my shoulder. With one hand, I fumbled the latch open on the pistol case, retrieved my gun, hammered the magazine home on my thigh, and looked at the front door. The calls and growls were still coming, and I didn't remember if I'd locked the bolt. My mind immediately jumped to the warning card left in my trailer, though I had no way to know if this was connected.

I took Kix to his bedroom, and laid him in his crib. Urgency replaced grogginess, and I rubbed my eyes with my left hand to speed up the process.

My house sat fifteen minutes from the interstate. In a nice, secluded, lake house community. Neighbors weren't close, so even if they were home they might not hear. Chances were, though, nobody was home. Most just vacationed here during the summer.

My gun was a Kimber Custom TLE II. A semiautomatic, double action .45. Stainless steel. No blued metal for Mr. August. I had grown used to it on the force, so I bought one of my own. I pulled the slide back to check the chamber, and let it snap home. We were safe. I was good with the pistol. Real good. And mad. Whoever was making noise outside and throwing things at my house was not safe.

In the spare bedroom, I peered out of the blinds.

Well, what do you know.

The resource officer stood there with two friends, laughing and bouncing rocks between his hands. While I watched, his short friend aimed and threw at the porch lights beside the front door. Thump. Missed. Several beer cans lay at their feet.

The RO was dressed in civilian clothes. Jeans and an untucked T-shirt. His short friend wore a vest and hat, the taller friend a Carhardt Jacket. All three had the build of former second-string varsity football players gone soft with beer and chips.

They were obviously drunk. Partly from the Natural Light, but also from the sense of power. Steve the RO was a police officer, and therefore somewhat above repercussion and given to being an idiot. I knew the feeling. Was I going to call the sheriff? Steve was the police. So to speak. Who would the sheriff trust? His fellow cop? Or me? Steve's friends felt invulnerable standing beside him. I smiled, and went to get my video camera.

A few minutes later, I opened the front door. The RO hit the short buddy on his shoulder with the back of his hand, and all three called louder with laughter. The laughter stopped when I stepped into the light and they saw my pistol pointed at them. The slight sound of the safety being thumbed off was effective. My gun was stainless, so it caught the porch light glare. You can't practice that. Takes talent. I left both the front door and screen door open and I stepped onto the lawn.

"Howdy, Steve," I said. "It's two a.m. on a Friday night, and you're throwing rocks at my house. What gives?"

Drunk courage disappeared. Almost always happened that way. Human nature shied away from danger. The three men on my lawn squirmed, vulnerable before the barrel.

I lowered the gun.

"Big city boy," he called back, "put'cher gun away. We ain't here to shoot. Put it away."

"I assume you fine country dumbasses are lost?" I said. "Go for a drive and forget where you are?"

"Put away the piece, August."

"You sure?"

"Yeah, we're sure," he said. His fingers twitched.

"If you go for a gun, I'm putting one in your knee. Got it?" I said.

They didn't move.

"Lovely night." I risked a glance at the stars. "You fellows bring the champagne?"

He cursed at my reasonable champagne suggestion, and spat.

"You gotta beatin' comin', city boy," Steve said. His consonants were slurred. "Put the gun down and take it like a man."

"The beating is inevitable?" I asked.

"Yep."

"That's very alarming, Steveo. I'm discouraged."

"Threw my cuffs back at me," he grumbled. "Tell'n me 'No.' Threatin' me, sonuvabitch. Threatenin' me! I'm the law!" He pointed at himself with his thumb. "Tellin' me I don't know how to spell."

"I told you I was sorry, Steve. And I meant it. You were just doing your job. I don't want to fight you. Go take a nap in your car."

"Initiation," he said.

"What?"

"Tha's what you got comin'. An initiation."

"Into your boys club?" I said.

"Into the South," his vest-wearing buddy said. He spit. I wished they wouldn't spit on my lawn so much. He was chewing tobacco. Nasty habit. Makes you spit on people's lawns. Vest-Buddy looked as though he was usually mad, didn't matter at what. I was convenient. "You don't belong here, asshole."

"Put 'way the gun. You disrespected me." Officer Steve Reed stumbled over the word. Said it like, "dispectretd me." "You disrespected the law. You got it comin'."

"You're high as a kite, Steveo," I said. "And about as intelligent."

He looked at me stupidly.

"Smoked up? Marijuana? Are you high?"

He glared. Stupidly. Maybe that's all he had.

"How do you know where I live?"

"I'm the police!" he yelled, spittle flying.

I shrugged and tucked my pistol shallowly into the back of my jeans. Steve wasted no time and went for his. He was slow and sloppy. Before he could get his hand behind his back, my gun was out again and aimed at him. The hammer drawing back sounded awesome in the silence.

"Toss your gun to me," I said. "Now. If your piece points at me, I'm firing. Straight into your chest. Understand? Toss me your gun."

He obeyed slowly, and it landed at my feet. His police issue, which showed intelligence. He'd have documentation for his qualification, potentially skirting legal trouble if he shot me.

"Anyone else?" I asked.

They shook their heads.

I fired into the tree behind them. The roar shocked all of us, even me and I knew it was coming. They nearly fell over.

"Jesus, August, what the hell!"

"I'll ask again. You boys got a gun?"

"No, we ain't got nothing else, damn it."

I flicked the thumb safety on my Kimber, retrieved his pistol, and placed both it and mine on the wooden stairs leading to the front door. Risky. But they were drunk. Not that risky.

"Okay," I said. "Come on, fatties. Come try to hit me with your big fat hands."

Steve licked his lips and grinned. The three of them approached, fanning out slightly. Denim zipped and zopped audibly as they moved. No more talking. Their confidence was restored, three on one, no guns.

"Or, you can walk away," I said. "That'd be the smarter move. I used to do this for a living. And for fun."

Vest-Buddy snickered.

Steve didn't say anything else, but threw a slow right hook at me. I had plenty of time to weigh my options. I could evade and counter, but I had to make this look good, and he was throwing with his arm rather than shoulder. So I ducked my head and let him hit me just above the forehead. His knuckles hit the extremely thick bone of my skull, which is a dome and therefore very hard and well supported. I heard his hand crack and maybe even fracture. People never expect that. My vision dimmed and I rocked backwards but steadied immediately. Steveo, on the other hand, grabbed his wrist with a howl and staggered away.

He was out of business for twenty seconds at least. Now it was two on one.

Tall Guy was already getting behind a punch. I shoved him off balance with my right hand and grabbed the second guy by his vest with my left. He swung. I ducked and punched him in the stomach hard enough with my right hand to take the wind out of him and double him over, and then brought my knee into his face. He toppled backwards, blood spilling out of his nose.

Tall Guy was on me again. I caught his punch with my left forearm and rammed the heel of my right hand into his teeth. His lip split. I kicked him in the crotch and he went down, holding himself.

Steve had his injured hand gingerly tucked to his chest and reached for something on his belt with the other. I backhanded him across the face. He collapsed.

He had been going for his clipped Buck knife. How would I have passed the time waiting for him to open it and threaten me?

All three were passed out. It was late, they were very drunk, and the violence had simply been too much. They'd most likely sleep the rest of the night.

I emptied the RO's magazine and confiscated the chambered round before stuffing it back into his belt.

The yellow Mustang in my driveway was registered to Steve Reed. Beer cans and candy wrappers littered the back seat. The bumper had a small, white, oval sticker with an "H" for Hatteras. I found a few pairs of handcuffs in the trunk.

"Mr. August, you are a naughty man," I said.

23

Our school office had an entire wall full of little wooden mailboxes for its staff. I checked mine on the way out the door, Monday. All I had was a little yellow slip of paper, informing me that I'd missed a call. I read the name twice.

"This who I think it is?" I asked the secretary.

"Mackenzie Allen's mother?"

"Yeah."

"Yes. She called about an hour ago and is hoping you can visit her after work. I wrote the directions on the back."

"Can't imagine me being much comfort to a grieving mother," I said.

"Maybe she just wants to look at that great butt she keeps hearing about," the guidance secretary called from the adjacent room.

The school secretary tried not to smile and said, "If you're going, would you take a few sympathy cards we signed for her?"

"I don't know why you're smiling," I said, accepting the cards. "It *is* great."

Mackenzie Allen's mother lived on the western end of Mecklenburg County. Allen had grown up in Mecklenburg but went to Blue Stone Middle, rather than South Hill. I called Leta and explained the situation as I drove west on Highway 58 past Boydton and turned into an old but well-kept neighborhood. The houses were mostly brick ranches with very green lawns and old dignified trees shading the windows. Her house looked similar to the rest, fronted by a small porch wide enough to contain a hanging bench and a rocking chair. Ms. Allen sat in the hanging bench.

"I was hoping you'd come," she called as I walked up her sidewalk. "You're Mr. August, right?"

"That's me," I said, and offered my hand. "Call me Mack."

"Just like my boy. Call me Debbie."

"I can see where Mackenzie Allen got his smile," I said.

"I heard you were a charmer," she said. "And I heard about your accent. Where are you from?"

"Louisiana, for the first ten years."

"It's a very attractive accent," she said, and patted the bench next to her. I sat.

She'd been gardening. Her Reeboks were dirty, a pair of gloves was draped over the bench arm, and her jeans bore grass stains. She looked fifty and like she'd just gotten over a few days crying. She took the sympathy cards from my hands.

"South Hill Middle," she said and she shook her head. "What a nice bunch of people."

"I think so."

"Were you at the funeral?"

"Yes ma'am," I said.

"I was pretty noisy, huh?"

"Nobody minded."

"Hah," she said, and elbowed me lightly. "Better not."

"I was impressed by the turnout."

"Not me. Mack was a good kid and everybody liked him. Plus, it was a sudden...interesting death. Always draws a bigger crowd."

"I met him about a month ago. Really liked him. We were going to play cards."

"Yep." She nodded. "Sounds like my Mackenzie. Loved cards."

"I like your garden."

"It gives me something to do, you know. Takes my mind off things. I think I have a few more days of sad left in me before I start working again. I'm a teacher too, you know. Blue Stone Elementary."

We sat in silence for a minute or two. She seemed very comfortable and so was I. I'd always been good with silence. She kicked her feet back and forth and rocked the bench. The chains creaked on the backswing.

"You found his body," she said after a while.

"I did."

"I bet that was scary."

"A little. I've some experience with bodies."

"Detective Andrews told me you used to be a police officer."

"Yes ma'am."

"What did you do?"

"I started out as a highway patrolman and then joined the Los Angeles Police Department. Later I was appointed to the Criminal Investigation Department."

"He said you were a detective?"

"In the Homicide Division."

"Why'd you quit?"

"Too many reasons."

"He said that when you quit it made the newspaper. That you were kind of famous."

"I worked a few highly publicized cases," I said.

"Were you good?"

"My sergeant thought so."

"That was nice of him."

"I put a lot of people in jail," I said. "Made him look tough."

"Detective Andrews said you were going to investigate my Mackenzie's murder."

"I'm going to help. Poke my nose around, see if I can find anything the police don't."

"I'd like to pay you," she said.

"No ma'am."

"I thought you'd say that," she said. "You seem the proud type."

"I told Andrews and myself that I would help. I'm helping because there's a killer that needs to be locked up. And because I liked Mackenzie. Not because of money."

"But don't some retired detectives work for money?"

"Private detectives, yeah. But I'm not one," I said.

"I'd still like to pay you."

"I work for free."

"But I want him found," she said and her face collapsed into tears and grief. She buried her face into my chest and hit me lightly with her fist. "I want him found, I want him found, and locked up or electrocuted. It's not fair, it's not fair," she repeated over and over. I hugged her shoulder. "It's too hard. Too hard that Mackenzie is dead and I don't know why or who." We kept swinging silently for another couple minutes. Her shoulders gradually quit shaking. I could picture her son climbing the tree in the front yard when he was younger. She sat up and wiped her eyes. "I'm tired of crying," she said. "But I have to know why he died. Please find out."

"Yes ma'am," I said.

T hird period was my first planning period. I loved planning periods. My feet went on my desk, I popped a can of Pepsi, downed a bag of Frito Honey Twists, checked a couple of my favorite internet news sites, and then afterwards did actual work. Computer whiz Mr. Cannon had shown me how to bypass the school firewall so I could check my other email account or play games on the internet, so sometimes no actual work was done. That happened only intermittently, however, as most days I prided myself on being a standup guy. Mackenzie August, man of integrity. Most days.

Christina sat at her desk, working on a study sheet. She was like many girls in the eighth grade: perky, loud, mouth full of braces, getting used to herself. Her parents were concerned about her grades, and so she sat in my classroom and corrected her test rather than play basketball in gym.

"Done, Mr. August," she said, and she brought me her paper. I inspected it. I'm a trained investigator, after all.

"Christina," I said slowly.

"Yes."

"Did you know I'm a trained investigator?"

"Mr. August, please," she said, and bounced up and down. "I want to go to gym."

"Christina," I said again. "These are all correct."

"Yes!" she yelped, raised her hands and ran out the door. "Thank you, Mr. August."

I finished my drink, threw the can into a bag I kept for recycling, and walked to the intercom panel. I buzzed the office.

The attendance secretary's voice came over the speaker. "Yes?"

"Can you tell Officer Reed that I'd like to see him when he's free? No rush, no emergency."

"Certainly."

My door opened a few minutes later. Officer Reed kept his hand on the doorknob, leaned halfway into the room and said, "Need something?"

"Steveo! What Hercules gave you that shiner?"

He tried to look passive and professional, but color rose into his face. Under his right eye sat a purple-green bruise and his face was swollen around it. His hand on the doorknob was wrapped in a soft splint.

"Me. It was me," I said. "Only now remembered. I hit you. It was awesome."

"Mr. August," he said. "What do you need?"

"I want to show you something. Have a seat."

I sat in one of the student desks and motioned for him to sit near me. He hesitated and then walked in and closed the door. I picked up a remote as he sat near me. A TV was sitting on a metal cart in front of us near the chalkboard.

"Check this out," I said, and pressed play on the remote. "Stick around, watch the whole thing. It's in your best interest."

The dark screen flickered and turned blue. Then the sound kicked in and my face appeared on the screen. The light was dim but my face was clear.

This is Mack August. Its two a.m., Friday night.

"Oh my god..." he whispered softly beside me.

There is yelling outside and rocks are being thrown at my house. I'm here alone with my nine-month-old son. I'm going outside and will attempt to videotape the encounter, in case something happens to me.

The camera was set down and the video was dark. Then the screen lit up, out of focus, as the blinds were raised and the front yard came into view. The picture focused and Steve and his buddies came into sharp relief.

"I don't want to give it away," I said. "But this is where the story gets good."

On the screen, I could be seen stepping onto the front porch, and the camera could also see my pistol. My words were clear, because I had intentionally spoken loudly. Most of Steve's words were clear, especially when he yelled. The footage indicated that he was drunk.

"Why are we watching this shit?"

"Shhh. This is my favorite part."

On screen, I said, *Straight into your chest. Understand? Toss me your gun.*

We watched.

I grunted as I was hit in the head onscreen. The camera caught me from my knees up, surrounded and attacked. It was great television.

"Pow, right in my forehead. That was a doozey. I didn't use a stunt double or anything, Steveo. That was me. And it hurt. You throw a mean right."

He said nothing.

The fight ended quickly. I tried not to swell with pride.

On screen, I walked back indoors and the screen went dark.

"Okay," I said. "I don't think you've seen this part."

The picture cut in again.

This is Mack August again. I was assaulted by three men, one of them armed with a loaded gun. They attacked me and I've been struck in the head. Fortunately they were drunk. I got lucky.

The camera was being carried down the lawn, away from the light, to the driveway. The camera stopped bouncing briefly, a light clicked on, and a small section of my yard became visible in the pale light.

The driver is drunk, and I don't want him driving away and killing someone. So, I cuffed them to the car.

The light fell onto the yellow Mustang. Steve lay facedown near the rear driver side tire. His arms were wrapped around the tire and handcuffed. That had taken a lot of work.

This is Steve Reed. He is a police officer. The resource officer at South Hill Middle School, where I work.

Steve swore again and called me a name that is inappropriate for an eighth-grade classroom. I should make him stand outside.

He brought two friends, threw rocks at my house, and told me he needed to beat me up. He brought his gun with him and attempted to pull it on me at one point. I don't recognize the other two guys, who are hand-cuffed to one another on my lawn.

When morning comes, they'll see the handcuff key in plain sight on the driveway. This way, they can't drive drunk and can't cause any more trouble tonight.

The camera turned around to face me.

This is Mack August. Going to bed.

The screen went dark.

"Be honest now," I said, and I hit Stop on the remote. "This is my first movie. Do you think it's good enough to make the evening news?"

"What do you want?" he said, voice dead, staring straight ahead.

"I think it might be good enough to make both Raleigh and Richmond's six o'clock news. They love stories with videos. An off-duty cop assaulting a civilian? With two of his buddies? Drunk? Caught on tape? With a baby inside? Two in the morning? This could be huge."

"What do you want, asshole."

"Huuuuuuge."

"Tell me."

"Information," I replied.

"What kind of information."

"You answer and I'll destroy the tape. That's the deal."

"What information," he said again.

"You smoke pot. I know it. You know it. I don't care. Probably making you stupider, but whatever. That's not what I'm after."

He said nothing.

"You knew that Mackenzie Allen smoked too." I was guessing, but his silence confirmed my suspicion. "I know you didn't kill him. I don't think you were involved. But I want to find out who is, so I'm chasing leads. He smoked. You smoked. And you knew he smoked. Right?"

He said nothing, but after a petulant moment he nodded.

"Progress. Here we go, Steveo. Here's what I think. All schools have marijuana getting into their hallways. I think you know how the pot is getting into this school. I don't think you're the dealer or supplier. But you know the source and you do nothing. Because it's your source too."

He said nothing.

"You're going to give me the name of your guy and where I can get him. You're not going to tell him I'm coming. In exchange, you get this tape and I forget you're an RO who smokes dope."

"No."

I stood and walked to my desk to retrieve a padded envelope. I set it in front of him.

"That envelope is addressed to the NBC news affiliate in Richmond. I'll address a few more to CBS and ABC, and also send copies to Raleigh. I'll send the tapes out today, along with a brief note giving the background," I said.

He squirmed in his seat, stood, and began pacing the room.

"What?" I said. "A week? Before you're fired? Not to mention assault charges. And you'll never wear a badge again."

He kept pacing and shaking his head, his hands on his belt.

"I lose my damn job either way," he said. He cursed and kicked my wall. "He'll rat on me. I know he will."

Rat. Too much TV.

"Not necessarily. I won't tell him I got him from you. If he tries to bring you into it, it'll be your word against his. You don't tell me, I send the tapes out."

He cursed again. The almighty F word.

"I apologized to you, Steve," I said. "A couple times. Then I gave you chances to walk away. You dug your own grave. I'm after Mackenzie Allen's killer. The only thing I can find on him is that he smoked pot. I am going to talk to his dealer. And you have to help me. Otherwise, I'm nailing you to the wall. That's all there is to it. Do the right thing. Help me catch the killer. If I can leave you out of the rest, I will."

"Why? Why are you doing this? Let the sheriff do his job."

"Mackenzie was my friend." And his mom asked me to.

"So what? He was my friend too. His death had nothing to do with grass, you hear me? Nothing."

He might be right. But I had to be sure. I said nothing.

He stopped pacing, laced his fingers and rested them on his head. Big sigh. He didn't look at me.

"Jon Murphy. He lives at 6 Nutcracker Lane, near Boydton. He was Mackenzie's guy too. He's connected. Don't mention me."

"Just say no to drugs, Steveo. Good advice."

Nutcracker Lane ran less than a quarter of a mile long, providing service to a mere three houses. Jon's house was a ranch with a concrete carport. Poorly trimmed boxwoods underneath windows with red shutters.

I watched his house for an hour until he came home around seven in an off-white Cadillac. A girl got out of the passenger side and they walked in through the front door. I popped Pringles, watched the second hand on my watch tick for thirty minutes, and thought about drugs.

I didn't have enough information to know if Jon ranked in the big leagues. At least one law enforcer had a healthy respect for him, which meant he probably had a good system, good reputation, good product, and maybe both muscle and connections. However, he lived in Mecklenburg County, the poorest county in the state. He could be the biggest thing in South Hill and still rank small time.

Someone in the county was dealing both crack and crank. I thought I detected early signs in a few students, and definitely saw it in a handful of parents. Jon's house didn't look like a meth lab, but the county in general felt like a good place to make it. It was both the poorest county and also one of the biggest, with a small police presence. Prime conditions.

Time. I tilted my head back and squeezed a few drops out of an eye-dropper into the corners of my eyes and held them there. I got out of the car, wiped away the tears, took a deep breath, put on my Ray-Bans and began walking unsteadily to Jon's house.

His wooden front door was ajar and I could hear voices inside. I banged on the screen door and put my hand on the bricks underneath his porch light.

The wooden door creaked open a little further and a guy peered out.

"The hell you want?"

"Hey man," I said. Heavy breathing. "Sorry to bother you at home, Jon. I just need whatever you got."

"Do what?"

"Listen, I'm on my way out of town, man, and I need to fill up before I go."

"Got the wrong house, dude," he said and began to close the door.

"Hey," I said. "No, dude. Jon. I'll get outta here fast. I got money. I brought money, man."

The porch light came on and he opened the door further to look at me.

"I don't even know you. You got nerve on you, dickhead, come here banging on my door." He had the typical South Hill accent. He was about my height, which was tall, and other than the sparse mustache he was a good looking, well-groomed guy. His hair was combed backwards and held there with gel. He wore khaki shorts and a polo shirt.

"I'm sorry, man. Haven't been here in years, just don't know where else to go this side of town. On my way to Boydton."

"Take off your glasses," he said.

"What? No."

"Take off your damn glasses, or take a hike. Think I'm scared of you cause you're big?"

"I brought money, man," I said, and stuck my hand inside my zip-up hoodie. "Look."

He opened the screen door wide enough to reach out and snatch the glasses off my face. I winced as light hit my sensitive eyes, and I looked at him.

"Whoa." He grinned. "You're pretty toasted, big fella."

"Nah, man, I brought money."

He smacked my fingers away from the zipper, and with a quick motion unzipped my jacket the rest of the way. He had strong hands. Five stacks of twenty-dollar bills fell out and landed on the front step. I had almost emptied my meager life savings, and it lay there between us. Jon didn't know me, but he recognized $2,500 bucks when he saw it.

"Holy..." I said, fumbling for and missing the money as it fell out of my jacket.

"Jeez man," he laughed again. "Pick that crap up, and get in here."

I bent down, groped for the thick wads of money, and walked in holding the cash close to my chest. His living room was arranged around an enormous flatscreen TV. New orange couches surrounded a thick glass coffee table. Two towers of DVDs stood next to his stereo system. Speakers were in the corners, and old cups cluttered on top. His walls were mostly bare except for a poster of girls in bikinis looking over their shoulders at the camera and holding beer. Jon had too much money and no decorating sense.

The girl sat on one of the couches. She wore wedge shoes, a short denim skirt, red tank top, and glasses that pushed her dyed blonde hair backwards. She smacked gum and looked annoyed.

"Just be a minute, baby," Jon told her. "Gotta do some business real quick."

"Thanks, man," I said again. I was sizing Jon up as quickly as I could. This was gonna go fast and I'd have one pass, maybe two at detecting a lie. "I'll be gone in no time."

"So what do you want? I don't keep much here."

"Everything," I breathed out. "Whaddaya got?"

"Nothing hard. I don't do that crap. Mostly cannabis, baby. I got reefer, oxycontin, E, shrooms, what?"

"No dice?"

"Nothing hard, I said. No heroin. No crystal."

"Lemme get two grand in bud, man. And five hundred Molly."

"No problem, man. Sit tight." Jon winked at the girl as he walked out. Easy to stiff the stoned.

"Jon's great, man." I smiled at the girl. "Good reputation. Great rep. Always there for you. Always there, you know?"

She gave me a fake smile and looked away.

As far as drug dealers went, Jon didn't appear that skeezy. His girl didn't have any bruises I could see and he was neither stoned nor drunk. He was, however, probably going to try to take my $2,500 and give me $1000 worth of drugs. He was also probably the one giving eighth-grade kids marijuana to sell to their friends.

Nothing hard. That was disappointing. Busting a cocaine dealer felt great. Busting a methamphetamine dealer felt better.

"So where do I know you from, bro?" he asked as he walked back in. He held two plastic grocery bags in his hand.

"Ah, dude, jeez," I said, and rubbed my forehead. "Been here twice, I think. Can't remember. Shame about Mackenzie, man. Frickin' shame."

"Mackenzie?" he said, and looked up.

"Yeah," I said, and let my shoulders drop. "Mackenzie Allen."

"Yeah," he said. "Yeah, man, it is a shame. Damn shame. You know Mackenzie?"

"Hell yeah, I knew Mackenzie. Maybe you seen me there at his funeral."

"Naw, I didn't get there. I should have." He stopped digging in the bag and looked into space. "I should have. Known Mackenzie for... hell, six or seven years."

"Me too, man," I said. I wiped my eyes and put my sunglasses back on. "Such a sweet guy. Solid. Ever play poker with him?"

"Yeah. At Greg's place. Maybe that's how I know you."

"Mackenzie, man. He was solid. Sweet guy. Who'd hurt Mackenzie?" I said. With my glasses on, I could watch him easily.

"Got no idea," he said and started digging. "You're so right, though. He was righteous. Righteous dude. I hope they catch him, you know? Hope they fry him. Hope they fry that guy's ass up like bacon."

"You don't know?" I said. "Man, I thought you'd know. About who got Mackenzie? You know everything, you know. Everyone always says. Murphy knows. Thought you'd know."

"I wish I knew, bro," he said. He was pulling out thick sandwich bags full of marijuana. "I wish I knew. I wouldn't let the cops get him. You get me? I'd put his ass in the ground myself. No cops needed, if I knew."

He was telling the truth. His voice was easy, he talked while he worked, didn't mind looking me in the eye, spoke with sincerity. His girl wasn't nervous, didn't start kicking her feet, didn't look at him out of the corner of her eye. My gut spoke with the experience of several years of interrogation. Jon the drug dealer knew nothing about the murder. Dang.

"Thought Murphy would know, for sure. Who'd know, then? Someone did it. Someone knows. If not you, then who would know, I wonder."

"Dunno, big guy. Lou would know. Lou always knows. Anytime something goes down, Lou knows."

Lou! I wondered if Andrews would know the name.

"Except Lou's been in jail for eight months now, I guess," Jon said.

Double dang. Lou don't know. My work here was done.

"Well..."

I dialed 911 on my phone, hit the speaker button and held it up in the air.

Jon looked up as the sound of ringing filled the room. Only one ring.

"911, what's your emergency?"

A bomb could not have changed the mood in the room quicker.

"What the hell..." Jon looked at the phone, smile gone.

"Help, help," I said in a slow, monotone voice. "I'm at 6 Nutcracker Lane, in South Hill."

"Johnny," the girl said in alarm, crawling up to sit on the back of the couch.

"Hey," Jon said, stupefied by the sudden shift of my voice and the conversation.

"I'm being attacked by Jon Murphy," I said. "Send help. Quickly."

"6 Nutcracker Lane, South Hill, Virginia," the feminine voice said over the phone. "Sir, can you verify that? I'm dispatching the police right now."

"That's the right address," I said helpfully, and hung up.

Stunned silence. The girl had quit chewing her gum. Jon's hands hung limp by his side, still holding bags.

"You know," I said, and zipped the wads of money back up in my jacket. "I'll probably hold onto these."

"Hey! The hell, man?" Jon yelled and hurled a bag at me. I let it bounce off my shoulder. It was filled with leaves and I'm super tough. "That ain't funny, man! Was that a joke? You joking, man?"

"Fraid not, Jon. You give drugs to kids. In fact, you probably give drugs to kids that are in my class. But not after today."

"Kim," he said and threw the grocery bags at her. She missed them in surprise and bags of pot fell over the back of the couch. "Start flushing, baby. Down the toilet. Go!"

"Johnny," she yelled.

"Now! You want me to go to jail, Kim? Is that what you want? My ass in jail?" he yelled back and went for his gun. I'd guessed he kept his piece hidden within the drawer of the couch's side table. I was right. When thinking straight, he wouldn't shoot me. But he probably wasn't thinking straight, so I got to the table at the same time and took his gun away from him. I grabbed his hand as he snatched the revolver, bent his wrist backwards until he was aiming at himself, and then twisted a little more until he yelled and let go. I threw it in the corner behind me.

I knew what was coming and had prepared for it, even hoped for it. I needed to take the charge, draw a foul, earn a good bruise. He swung at me. I stood my ground and didn't block him. I turned my face at the last minute to take the punch but not lose my face. His knuckle caught me on the lip and split it open. Perfect.

I turned my body into a low uppercut that drove under his ribs. Not enough to injure him. I no longer hurt people for fun. Just enough to keep him from cleaning my clock. He groaned and staggered backwards.

Outside, the clear wail of police sirens sounded impossibly near. I had just hung up. Kim hadn't even left the room.

He rushed me, trying to bowl me over. I pivoted and automatically raised an elbow, but stopped before I drove it into his face. He was supposed to be attacking me, not the other way around.

My hesitation cost me. The world turned white as he struck me on the side of the head. My glasses landed near my feet. The sirens sounded as though they were on our street.

"Jon," I growled. "I am annoyed."

He spit at me and attacked a last time. I turned again, used his momentum and threw him into the couch so hard it turned over. I retrieved my glasses and walked out the front door.

Three cars so far. Four deputy sheriffs streaming from the doors and running toward Jon's house. The front lawn flickered with blue lights. I raised my hands. The deputies apparently recognized me because they ran straight by and into the house. I was notorious.

Sheriff Mitchell stood next to his car and put down his radio as I approached. Andrews stood beside him.

"Took long enough," Mitchell said. "Been waiting two hours."

"A girl is in the back, doing her best to flush bags down the toilet," I said.

Andrews repeated that into his radio, and said, "She won't get far." He nodded toward my bleeding lip and said, "Nice one."

"Badge of honor," I said. "Taking a bite out of crime."

"Thanks for getting us in," he said.

"Mackenzie August, professional victim."

"Pressing charges?"

"Nah. And I don't think he had anything to do with Mackenzie Allen."

"Wanna stick around anyway?"

"Nope," I said, anxious to scoot before a newspaper reporter showed. "Take my statement, then I'm going to play with my son before bedtime. You're not invited."

L eta met me at the door the next morning in her cooking apron. Kix inhaled, rocked in my arms and held out his arms to her.

"Well." She laughed, which she always did. "Look who's a happy boy today." She always said that too. She took Kix. "I heard about you on the news this morning."

"Oh yeah?"

"Channel Eleven. That's my favorite. James don't like the other shows much. The reporter, she's that blonde I like, was talking about a bust at a drug house. She said the same person who discovered the dead fellow named Mackenzie was the one who called the police to the house with the drugs."

"Gracious," I said, and set Kix's diaper bag inside the front door. "It's not even eight in the morning yet."

"So it was you? James said it probably was, which is why you were out so late last night."

"It was me. Tonight, though, I plan on no drug busts. I'll be here to get Kix on time."

"Ah, its no trouble," she cooed, and bounced Kix. "It likes to stay with us." She also called Kix "it" quite a bit.

The Mecklenburg County Sheriff's Office sat several miles out of my way in Boydton but I made the trip anyway. The office was functional and old, clean and efficient. Filing cabinets, telephones, old computers, wooden bead-board walls. I saw a poster which read, "Crime of the Week." The latest entry was five years ago. Puppies had been stolen.

I spoke with one of the deputies who'd been there last night and then pushed into the jail. Four cells, only one of them occupied. Murphy sat on his cot with his back leaning against the painted cinderblock wall.

"Can't believe it," he said, watching me. He had bags under his eyes and his hair looked greasy. Rough night. "I can't fucking believe you're a middle school teacher."

"During the day. At night I wear a cape and fight crime."

"What the hell are you doing here?"

"I was going to ask you the same question," I said. "Classy guy like you, in a place like this?"

Murphy swung off of the cot and walked over to the bars. He threaded his arms through and leaned against the metal.

"Why you standing so far back? Prima donna. Worried about getting hit?"

"Heavens yes," I said. "If I stand this close will you hit me?" I asked, and got a little closer. "This close? Thiiiis close?"

"Think you're funny?"

"I'm glad you asked. I really, really do. Wit is educated insolence, you know."

"I get out on bond soon," he sneered. "You won't be laughing then." I gave him credit. It's difficult to appear tough while standing behind bars looking at your captor.

"Let me save you some bruises. Even if you bring a friend you can't take me."

"Yeah right. Your ass is mine."

"Honest to goodness. Not trying to brag," I said and held up my hands in what I hoped was my "Look how honest I am" stance.

"How do you know?"

"I used to fight competitively for a couple years. Cage matches." I shrugged. "I took one on the kisser from you, and now I know I could take several of your best shots and keep ticking. You couldn't take one of mine. Just the way it is."

"Why are you here?"

"Came to apologize."

"You gotta be kiddin' me."

"Nope. For real. I'm glad you're behind bars. I'm not sorry I put you there. But I feel a little bad about lying to you."

"You're messed up, man. Sick in the head, get it? Messed up."

"I'll bring lunch, make it even. Tell me where and I'll buy."

"Go to hell, man. Think that makes us even?"

"Probably not, drug dealer. Probably not," I said, and turned to leave.

"You're the ugliest damn teacher I ever saw."

Ouch.

TESTING DAY AT SCHOOL. Subject-verb agreement assessment. I had a feeling the scores were going to be brutal. However, the classes were quiet all day as the students took the test and passed notes afterwards. A handful of students inquired about the source of my busted lip. Taylor's class was testing also, so she emailed me dirty jokes all day and made suggestive comments. The guidance counselor stuck her head in twice to pull out students she suspected were still struggling with the murder.

My mailbox in the office contained a few notes asking me to call the local newspaper for an interview. The drug raid was receiving exaggerated coverage because of the recent murder and potential connections. The local, small-time newspaper ran the story every day, including a grainy picture of me smiling for the yearbook photographer. I received emails from teachers who read the paper and wanted details. I told them I'd only answer if they bought me corndog nuggets from the cafeteria. I grew tired of being famous, but corndog nugget day made everything better.

The agriculture class, led by Roy the agriculture teacher, dug holes around my trailer and planted bushes. I wondered if I should be offended. A clog of dirt hit the window now and then, and I'd have bet someone a dollar Roy started it. He was still angry over Taylor's interest in me.

The aching in my lip forced me to ponder the ethics of yesterday's bust. Not exactly entrapment, but neither was it the most honest way of bagging a dealer. If Murphy's lawyers got nasty, we had a picture of me with a busted lip and a picture of him spotless. Chances were good, though, that a plea bargain would be reached quickly. Not a lot of wiggle room for the culprit, he was caught red-handed.

During my planning period, some unknown force propelled my steps in a meandering search around parts of the school where I had not yet ventured. Eventually I wandered into Mr. Suhrs room. I'd met him only once, the giant in the workroom. His classroom was more like a large workshop. Something masculine deep inside of me grunted. His students worked in groups, building small robots capable of obeying simple commands. The groups were deep in thought and conversation. Mr. Suhr came to lean beside me on the windowsill.

"I wondered when you'd come see me," he said. He still possessed a great smile and short, shocking white stubble beard. I hadn't learned much about him. He'd been teaching at the school for as long as anyone could remember; Kristen Shortt thought he drove a van for the local YMCA after school; Mr. Charlie said he went to a local church. Everyone respected him, that was certain.

"Didn't know you'd been waiting."

"Not waiting. Only curious." He put one of his great big arms around my shoulders and gave me a side hug. Which was weird. "I know you are under quite a bit of stress, my friend. How are you feeling?"

"Blue, I suppose," I said. "I'm always a little down after action."

"I heard about you on the news."

Several of his students were also my students. As they saw me, they called out or waved. I waved back.

"You're popular, you know," he said. "They all like you."

"Means bupkis unless they pass their SOLs."

"Doesn't mean bupkis. Means you're making a difference."

"Aw shucks."

"Nervous?" He grinned. "About the SOL tests?"

"Seems like the students don't care, most days."

He laughed that big, warm laugh of his, and said, "It will be okay. We all feel like that. Most days." We watched them work silently for a few minutes, and then he said, "Do you know why you risked your life yesterday?"

"Not much risk."

"But a little."

"Yeah," I said. "A little. Trying to do the right thing, I guess. Help catch a killer."

"That is not your job anymore," he said.

"I'm good at it." I shrugged. "And I'm used to it."

"So?"

"You saying I shouldn't help?"

"No, no. Not at all, my friend. You are big for a reason."

"What does that mean?"

He smiled and didn't answer.

"What's your point?"

"I think that even if you were not good at it, or not used to it, you would be looking for a way to help."

"So?" I said.

"My question is...do you know why?

"Do you?"

"I think so." He nodded

"Save me some time. Tell me."

"Guilt."

"Guilt," I repeated.

"Yes," he said.

"What do I feel guilty about?"

"You are under tremendous guilt," he said. "Because you think you have failed God."

I took my time answering, stunned at the man's boldness. Everyone around here seemed to be a baptist, but Mr. Suhr was one of the few who talked about it. Even working for a church, God hadn't always come up regularly. Why do these things make us feel awkward?

"How's that?" I asked.

"You feel guilty," he said. "Because you think you have failed Him. And you feel angry, because your self-image has only gone downhill since you began to follow Him. And you feel guilty about feeling angry."

"Got me figured out, huh."

He smiled and hugged me again with the arm that still rested around my shoulders.

"No," he said. "I listen. And watch."

"Listen? To what?"

"You. Not necessarily your words, though. And I listen to our Creator."

"Mr. Suhr," I said. "I'm not used to conversations like this. Not even when I worked at a church. No one talks like this."

"However," he said. "When is the last time a conversation stirred your soul as much as this?"

I couldn't say anything. So I didn't.

"Before you leave, you must promise to return. And talk with me."

"Sure."

"Good, then I will tell you this. You have not failed Him. You, Mack, are very loved. And you are doing great."

I turned and walked out of the room, heart pounding.

No golf practice, home early for a change. We went for a jog around our neighborhood. Fall was beginning to mature. The leaves were not yet brilliant but the sun had lost its sting. A breeze blew in from the lake and pushed around the lofty tree branches shading us as I pounded up and down the hills around our house, Kix quietly watching in his jogging stroller. Moving to this neighborhood continued to prove healthy for me mentally, physically, and emotionally.

Every time I replayed the tape of my conversation with Mr. Suhr, my chest tightened and I had to fight off crying. I felt as though he'd tapped into waters I didn't know existed, and I couldn't suppress them.

I'm a softy.

Afterwards, while I prepared dinner, Kix sat in his playpen and inserted plastic coins into a musical piggy bank. My son kept passive-aggressively telling me I needed to sharpen up our finances. I took two steaks out of the fridge and was grinding in salt and pepper when the front door opened.

"All the August boys," my father said, dropping his travel bag onto the couch. "Under one roof."

Kix just about hyperventilated.

27

"Has your principal reviewed you yet?"

"She observed class a week ago. No warning. Then went over it with me last Friday."

"Good review?"

"Yes," I said. Kix sat in my father's lap and kept guessing which big hand his pacifier was hiding in. He smiled but it looked like a really frustrating game to me.

"Think you'll be back here next year?" he asked.

"Nope."

"Nope?"

"I'm moving back to Roanoke over the summer. Our family is so small, we gotta stay in the same city."

"I like your thinking."

We had finished our salads, steaks and iced tea, and sat at the dinner table fat and happy.

"This has been good for you, hasn't it?"

"Extremely."

"Ever fully figured out why you moved to California in the first place?" he asked me.

"I think so."

"Let's hear it."

I poured myself some iced tea, took a drink, and collected my thoughts.

"Mom died that spring. I was demoted to second string during training camp in July. Krystal moved to New York in August, and we were having problems. Then she died in September. That was a rough year."

"Duwayduway," Kix said, holding two of his grandfather's fingers in his little fists.

"Looking back on it, I'm embarrassed to say that the move to California was probably most influenced by the demotion on the football team. I found my self-worth in the eyes of the people I impressed with superficial achievements. When that faltered, so did my worth to the world and to myself. I became less of a man."

"In your own eyes."

"And probably in no one else's," I agreed. "Krystal tried telling me that, but I assumed she valued me less too. I think most of our fights were based on my insecurity."

To my father's credit, he managed to keep from nodding.

"I moved to California to get away from the eyes in which my insignificance reflected. And to impress those eyes from afar. I'm still not sure exactly whose opinion I valued so much or who I was trying so hard to impress. Teammates, coaches, teachers, classmates who wanted me to sign their hats, girls I suppose."

"You're smarter than you look."

"I'm gorgeous, so that's saying something."

"How long did it take you to realize California would not bring relief?" Timothy August asked.

"Not long. Waiting in California was a whole new batch of eyes I needed to impress. That realization was horrible."

"I think you left something important out. Something you should probably know."

"What's that," I said.

"Graduation. You were graduating that fall. Don't underestimate the significance that oncoming date had in the back of your subconscious. The threat of growing up has done in mightier men than you. A lot of guys put off maturity by tying themselves to a snowboard, living on a mountain, and refusing to accept responsibility for anything after graduation."

"Running from responsibility, running from failure."

"Running from pain," my father said. "And running to adventure."

"A new proving ground."

"Keep in mind, son," he said. "Not all of your motives for running were cowardly or based on pain. A lot of them were natural and very understandable. The great challenge of your adolescence was football. And you conquered it for years, until that summer. Considering life was dog-piling you, it's not hard to understand why you ran to something else you could conquer. That stage of life is about adventure, hard work, independence, which you found in the Highway Patrol. You acted like a man."

"Maybe not the wisest man."

"Agreed. But the two most important women in your life had died recently. Acting out is realistic."

"You've thought about this a lot."

"Maybe more than you have," he said. "It's what dads do."

"So what's the next question?" I asked.

"What's your evaluation of your time in California? What was good, what was destructive, what was both."

Another drink of iced tea. My brain hurt. I hadn't talked this much in a while. I hadn't talked this much about myself in years. Every so often, though, we had this talk. I verbalized my mental processes, reflected on growth, admitted problem areas. He listened, commented, approved, and helped me mature. My conversation earlier with Mr. Suhr had left me raw and emotional, so I was using significant resources to abate tears.

"Highway Patrol was a good confidence builder. I was the best. Worked really hard, helped a lot of people, hurt a lot of bad people," I said. "My life was my job, though. Everything else suffered. I had nothing. No one cared about me, including myself, no hobbies. I'd take racing classes on my off days to become a better driver. No one wanted to ride with me. It got worse when I joined LAPD. I'd get up in the morning and go to the shooting range. If someone had better marks than me I couldn't sleep. During breaks I'd run or hit the weights. Took anything I could to make me faster, meaner, stronger. I attended martial arts classes at nights. Kung-fu, Jiu-Jitsu, Judo, karate, whatever I could fit in. Started fighting in cages. I never lost. Wouldn't sleep. Instead I'd go on stakeouts or bother informants. After injuries, the hospitals could never keep me as long as they wanted to."

"Wow, you're a mess."

"Ugh," I said. "It was terrible. An eight-year blur of pain and self-doubt. I won every award, got every promotion, slept with every girl I saw, drank all the time, beat all the people I wanted to beat. And all of it fell like bags of cement at my feet. Worthless, dead weight. Hollow. I was the most arrogant and insecure and lonely person I knew."

"Was anything positive?"

"Got to play a lot of golf. When I wasn't destroying myself."

"How's your game?" he asked.

"Eh," I said. "Can't get under a fifteen handicap. I enjoy coaching."

"What else was positive?"

"My partner, Richard. That was really positive. Other stuff too, strength, work ethic. Friends, like Manny. But mostly Richard."

"He was a good man." My father nodded.

"The best."

"And Kix," he said. Kix murmured in recognition. "Kix is positive."

"Whatever is better than positive," I said. "That's what Kix is."

"He crawling yet?"

"Nope, not sure if he ever will. Lucky he's cute."

"I never met Melynda," he said. "She must have been an attractive girl."

"A knockout. He looks like her. A lot. Have you never seen a picture?"

"No."

"I'll find you one. Kix would have had really attractive parents. In a lot of ways. I have a couple pictures in the box with Richard's stuff.

Haven't gone through it in a year, though. I don't even like that side of the closet. Too many emotions. I wish Kix could have met her."

I wiped tears off both cheeks and took another drink, wishing it was beer.

"Haven't thought about it in a while, huh," he said.

"Only objectively. And not often."

Kix was reclining in his grandfather's arms, sucking on his pacifier, watching me with concern. He grunted a question. I winked. He understood.

"And," I said. "Those seven years, eight years, whatever, were selfish and stupid and self-centered and destructive, but I've come out the other side stronger and ready to move on."

"Because you found religion."

"Because I found peace," I said.

"You know, son, just because I'm not religious doesn't mean I don't like that part about you."

"You know, Pop, just because I worked at a church doesn't mean I'm religious."

"What do you call it then?"

"I don't know. I don't go to church, I don't have any religious friends, I don't like the christian radio stations, I drink, I don't feel like baptists would like me anymore than I like them. I read but cannot understand the Old Testament. Sometimes," I said, and paused. "Sometimes I don't even think God likes me very much, though I know that's not true. Whatever that is, that's what I am."

"Wow," he said. "I bet you really were an awful preacher."

"Unbelievably bad. I went from being a self-destructive cop to the head of the youth outreach at a church in two weeks. I was awful."

"They must have been desperate."

"We both were."

"When is this little guy's bedtime?"

"Ten minutes ago."

"So am I a heathen?" he asked.

We sat on my dock in canvas folding chairs watching the water. The sun was setting earlier recently and would only be up another thirty minutes. We both wore bug spray. A baby monitor hissed quietly beside me.

"Going to hell?" he asked again.

"I don't know. I suppose that's up to you and Him."

"I'm a pretty good guy," he said.

"You're better than that. And a great father. But I don't know if that's what matters."

"I hope it is."

"I'm sure you do."

"Keep praying for me. Maybe I'll come around."

"Hm. Prayer. I should start that."

"Thanks for saying I'm a good father."

"Great father. And you're welcome."

I was getting ready to fill him in on the Mackenzie Allen murder investigation but I noticed that the jet ski I'd been watching was headed for our dock. The driver came in quickly but killed the engine and floated peacefully up to and nudged the bumper around the sides of the wood.

Taylor Williams stepped off the jet-ski and tossed a rope around the wooden pole, loosely securing her craft. She was dressed in running shoes, no socks that I could see, small black running shorts that showed off her tan athletic legs, and a white, long-sleeved T-shirt that hugged her chest. Her hair was back in a ponytail.

She put her hands on her hips and smiled at my father. I could get a tan from her smile.

"You're always here when I come around, aren't you," she said.

"Lucky me," my father said and stood.

"I'm Taylor."

"Hi Taylor. Nice to meet you again. I'm Mack's father."

"If the family resemblance continues another generation," she said, shaking hands, "then Kix will be the third handsome August in a row."

"I used to worry about Mack," he said and he sat back down. "He was an ugly baby."

Taylor somehow managed to perch on the arm of Dad's chair. Impossible to be comfortable, but she made it look good. She crossed her legs, and her arm went around his shoulders.

"I'm one of the many girls glad it didn't skip a generation," she said.

"Even with this new haircut?" he asked, pointing at me.

"Especially with. I've come to ask him out on a date with me."

"Modern woman," he said.

"No, just impatient. He's taking his sweet time."

"Never a bright boy," he agreed.

"Lucky he's so pretty."

I wondered if either of them could see me. I kept quiet, in case they couldn't. To kill time, I wondered how so many people knew where I lived.

"Is he busy tomorrow?"

"No ma'am. And I'm the babysitter."

"Brilliant," she beamed. "I'll email him directions. He can pick me up at two. We're going to a local hunt club."

"Which is what?"

"A few of my friends have a hunt club. Sort of like a building just for boys and their guns. Sometimes they invite us girls, but I'm boyless. So I'm borrowing Mack for the day. Tell him to bring his gun." She looked at me. "You do have a gun, don't you?"

"Just little ones."

"Disappointing. Even I have a pistol. Bring what you have. Maybe one of the other boys will play nice and let you borrow. You won't let him forget?" she said, and put her hand on Dad's shoulder.

"Never."

"Fabulous. Well, I'm off before the sun sets. You two won't watch while I bend over to unmoor my boat, will you?"

"No ma'am," he said.

"We'll probably just try to figure out what moor means."

"See you tomorrow." She smiled and skimmed back across the lake. Small waves lapped against the shore in her wake.

"Yowzah," my father said.

"Yup."

"Kinda hard to breathe when she's around."

"You should see her at work when she's not dressed so modestly."

"Going to keep practicing the tenets of your faith tomorrow night?" He grinned.

"I hope."

28

Taylor lived in a rented guest house that belonged to someone I could only assume was the king of another country, based on the size of the main house. Both sat on the northwest shore of Lake Gaston, opposite mine on the southeast side. The north shore was where all royalty vacationed, apparently.

I had no idea what to wear to a hunting party, so I decided to go rugged rather than regal. Boots, jeans, long-sleeved tee with a casual jacket to hide my shoulder rig. I only brought my Kimber .45. Taylor ducked into my car wearing sandals, white jeans, a blue Henley shirt, diamond earrings, cross necklace and a chunky white bracelet.

She looked at me, lit up the car with a smile, and said, "Hiya stranger."

"You should never get into cars with strangers." I smiled back. It felt pathetic next to hers.

"What about if he's handsome?" she asked.

"Not even if he has candy."

"You brought candy?" She sat up straighter, smile still going strong.

"It'd have been great if I had," I said.

"Even greater if you had a nice car."

"Now it's personal."

"I'm just being honest. You drive an old man's car," she said.

We sped away from the lake, northwest into Bracey on Blackridge. Our conversation revolved around students in our classes, and comparing horror stories. She complained about my car, complained about her car payments, and complained about our coworkers.

"Turn left here," she said. "Down this gravel road." I obeyed. "I think you'll probably be the only guy here without a truck."

"You mean the only guy not compensating?"

"You should tell them that." She arched an eyebrow.

"Sure. I enjoy fighting five guys at once."

The hunt club appeared to be a glorified shack in an evergreen clearing. Behind it, barely standing, was an even more dilapidated building, which Taylor called a skinning shed. I parked beside several trucks. If I looked way, way up I could see the door handles.

A girl came crunching across the gravel to hug Taylor hello.

"Well, well," she said, as she hugged Taylor's arm. "Who is the hunk?"

"He can hear you," Taylor whispered back.

"I don't care."

"This is my hunk. Mack. Mack, this is my best girlfriend from high school, Carla."

Carla was small and collected and stylish. Her smile seemed sincere and her eyes were warm. All of her clothes were stenciled with name brands.

"Mack, this is my husband Sam," she said, as a wiry, medium-built man walked up. Sam stood shorter than me. He was losing some of his light-brown hair, but even with all of his hair he wouldn't warrant Carla based on appearances. He looked like he was funny. I hoped not funnier than me. We were dressed similar.

He shook my hand.

"Hi Mack."

"Sam. Carla."

"You're, ah," he said, looking up at me. "You're a big guy."

"I pad my shoes."

"Still though. I'm a little intimidated."

"You want to feel his muscles?" Taylor asked.

Carla nodded. "Yes please."

"You may not feel my muscles," I told Sam.

"Well, now I want to."

The four of us walked to the shed. Taylor wrapped her arm around mine. I concentrated on keeping my feet falling one after the other.

Two guys stepped out of the hunt club. Big guys. As tall as me. Both had facial hair. Neither looked funny like Sam. At least I could wrap up second place in the funny contest.

"'Bout time, girlie," said the one with short hair and goatee.

Taylor squeaked, left me, ran with her arms up and hugged him. A lot of the eighth-grade girls in my class did the same thing to their boy friends. He hugged her back and shot me a look, like "See, my territory," before she left him to hug the other tall guy. Now I recognized the second tall guy. Roy, from school. The agriculture teacher. Not my biggest fan.

Tall Guy Number One inspected me. "So who's the new guy, girlie?"

"You can call me new guy," I said. "I like it."

"Funny guy."

"Even better."

"Aaron, this is Mack. Mack, Aaron," she said.

Aaron appeared to be a big, strong, lumbering fellow. He wore a red flannel shirt. Maybe he sold paper towels. He did his best to crush my hand in his. I did my best to hold back tears. He was almost, but not quite, as big as me.

Roy spared me a glance. "Didn't know you were coming."

"Every party needs a pooper."

Two more girls walked out of the shed. Neither looked particularly thrilled to be there, nor thrilled to see Taylor, nor did they introduce themselves to me.

"Mack, that's my wife, Pam," Aaron said. "The mean one."

"I like her already."

"And that's Roy's wife, Marie. The meaner one."

This was weird. Everything about it.

Taylor pulled me into the shed. The inside had dingy carpet, photos of deer carcasses hung, and a swinging lightbulb. Great place for a poker night. Odd place to call a club. Guns were collected within an open chest that stood in the corner.

"See? Very manly," she said.

"Think I should spit? Prove I belong?"

"Please don't. Isn't Aaron great? We used to go out."

"The greatest."

"Think you could beat him up?"

"I'm positive I can outrun him."

"Still think your dick is bigger than his?" she asked.

My date was so classy.

Carla walked in and wrinkled her nose at Taylor.

"Looks like Dumb and Dumber are in foul moods," she whispered.

"What else is new," Taylor said, and she explained, "The two wicked wives. We hate those bitches."

"Then why come?" I asked.

"For the boys," Taylor said. Of course. My uncomfortable meter was beeping faster. "Aaron is a lumberjack. A forester."

"Definitely can't beat him up."

"Why not?"

"I'm a teacher."

"Wuss."

I agreed.

Aaron and Roy played with their rifles and shot at targets for the next hour. I slowly figured out the scene.

Aaron and Roy invited Taylor to show off. The three of them went to high school together and old habits died hard. They invited their wives to keep them happy. The wives came to keep an eye on them and glare at Taylor. Taylor came to flirt with the boys and make the two wives jealous. Carla came to keep Taylor company and gossip about old friends. Sam came because he loved his wife and appeared to be just as uncomfortable as me. I was invited to...compete, I suppose? Taylor and the other girls sat up straight and applauded when one of the guys shot a can. Everyone except for the two gun-toting giants sat on a few blankets and ate crackers, cheese and chips. I moved away from my date so she'd quit trying to put food in my mouth. At least the sun was out.

I sat near Sam to test my funny skills. I liked him. Good guy. A website designer. He was funnier than me. I wondered how I could accidentally shoot him.

"Hey Mack," Aaron called. "Want to give this a try?" They had broken out clay pigeons and a hand trap to throw with.

"Oh yes," Taylor called. "He used to be a cop! Maybe he can shoot as well as you, Aaron."

"Well," Aaron chuckled. Clearly the notion was absurd. I didn't think Aaron's brain could handle such a ridiculous idea.

"C'mon, city boy," Roy said. "Got you a shotgun all loaded up."

I stood.

"Can you shoot?" Sam asked.

"I can probably miss my foot," I said. "So that's good."

The weeds around Aaron and Roy were littered with shells and cartridges. Taylor cheered and clapped as Roy handed me the gun. Double-barreled twelve gauge. I looked for the break release.

"Know how to work that?" Roy asked.

"Golly, I hope so."

"Loaded it up for you."

"You ready?" Aaron said. "Here we go."

He flung the trap forward and the spring-loaded arm launched the red clay disk high and far into the fall air. I raised the shotgun to my shoulder. Before I could zero in, a second pigeon followed.

I thumbed the safety off, which I believe disappointed them. He had thrown fast so I aimed fast, took a breath and held it.

Shotguns do not sound like the pleasant pop heard on television. Nor even the more realistic sounds at the movie theater. The deep-throated explosion scared you if you weren't used to it. The sound was felt as much as it was heard.

I pulled the trigger and the woods reverberated with the blast. The clay pigeon shattered.

I swung the barrel around onto the second disk. It was acting a little like a Frisbee, rising high and stalling a little. I still held the same breath. Shifted the selector and pulled the second trigger.

Click. Misfire. I wasn't surprised. Probably loaded a shell he suspected of water damage. Embarrass the new guy.

Before anyone could move I turned sideways, dropped the shotgun into my left hand and pulled out the Kimber .45 with my right. Pushed the safety off. Squinted.

The disc was really too far away for a pistol. And it was moving. My chances weren't good. One in three. I fired anyway. The pistol kicked slightly in my hand, and the disc broke into two pieces and fell back to earth. A slight breeze blew the heady smell of gunpowder smoke away from us as the gunfire echo faded.

"Beginner's luck," I said.

29

If Taylor got her wish, Aaron and I'd end up in a fistfight, and then she and I would wind up back at her place in bed. Unless I was misreading the signals. Which might as well have been painted on billboards.

We sat around two wooden outdoor tables at Kahills, a fun local restaurant off of I-85. Most of the South Hill proletariat saved Kahills for special occasions. Best food for fifty miles, and it had that great glowing polished wood atmosphere.

Candles burned in their stained glass vases and thin smoke collected in the wide canvas umbrella above. Both Aaron and his wife smoked. Roy had drunk himself into an angry silence. Taylor, Carla, Sam and I made small talk when the two girls weren't at the bar talking with the bartender, another old friend from high school. During that time, Sam and I debated Tony Romo's throwing motion and the potential difference in his earlier stats if Terrell Owens hadn't been on the team. Deep stuff.

I was sleepy. The time was approaching ten, for goodness sake, and it'd been a surreal day. Roy's wife Marie knocked her glasses off the table for the third time, and Roy told her that if she did that again he was going to break them. What a man. He stood.

"C'mon," he mumbled. "Let's go. M'tired."

"Roy," I said, and stood. "You've both had too much. I'll drive you home."

"Naw, I'm fine."

"You're not. You're drunk. I'll drive."

He stared at me through heavy eyes, and told me he could drive his own damn truck and I should go to hell. And I should mind my own business and keep my nose out of his ass, which struck me as an uncomfortable metaphor. His language earned looks from the surrounding tables.

He stumbled away and his wife followed, herself unsteady.

Sam said, "Drunk enough to kill someone."

"He won't get far. There's a patrol car hidden on 85 south."

"Should we warn him?"

"We'll visit him in jail."

A new song came over the speakers. A slow ballad by a girl country artist I didn't know.

"Come on, stud," Taylor said, and took my hand. "I picked the next two songs on the jukebox." We walked onto the makeshift dance floor that'd probably be housed for the winter within a month.

I wasn't drunk, but I was exhausted. Sometimes the effects are the same. I wasn't crazy about Taylor. But looking at her made my stomach flip. She was easily the most attractive person wherever she went. And I suspected she'd undone a few buttons on her shirt since we arrived. I demanded that my hand let go of hers but it overruled me. I told myself to quit following her but my body followed hers impulsively.

She walked past another slow-dancing couple, pivoted and pulled me near. I held her hand at my chest. Her other arm was around my waist. She was short compared to me and she fit in easily. My right arm circled her shoulders and my hand entangled itself into the hair at the nape of her neck. She smelled like flowery conditioner and an expensive night-out perfume. Her face nuzzled into the shirt across my chest and she smiled with her eyes closed. Our dance was not the dance of a first date.

We didn't move much, but rather let the world dance around us. The music droned in the background but the song was irrelevant. It only existed to slow time. She was well known, maybe even notorious, and we were getting a lot of attention. My mind vaguely recorded Aaron and his wife leaving, and then Sam and Carla. I was too tired to care. My list of concerns narrowed to my exhaustion and the girl pressed against me.

I don't remember when we started kissing. Our faces were touching, her soft lips kissing mine, arms around my neck, mine around her slim waist. My fingers craved her skin.

We left. She kissed my ear and my neck, and would have crawled into my lap if I let her. She breathed heavily.

"You'll be the biggest guy I ever fucked," she said.

I didn't comment. I fought against the storm raging inside and fought to keep my car on the road.

"I bet your dick is bigger than Roy's. I hope so. Hurry *up*."

She kept whispering into my ear, and somewhere between Kahill's and her house the spell she'd cast over me vanished. The more she talked the more she turned into a beautiful trash can. An open sewer with a great body.

We stopped in front of her house. I let the car engine run.

She crossed her arms, took the hem of her shirt in her hands, and pulled it off with one easy motion. Her bra was dark blue, a pushup, and the moonlight touched only the upper curves of her breasts.

"I want to be fucked, Mack. For an hour. We go until I say. Got it?"

I wanted to. It'd been a long time, over a year, and she looked fun. Visions of past conquests flitted through my memory, clouding judgement.

"Taylor..."

"You can tell people about it. Fucking me is a big deal."

"I can't do this."

She put her hand in my lap and squeezed. "I beg to differ, big boy. Wow."

She opened the door and got out. She undid the top button of her jeans. It parted with an audible pop of cloth. I could no longer see her face, only her hips, her hands, her navel.

I can't do this.

Yes you can. Best hour you've had in months.

Maybe, but I'll pay for it.

Go inside. Take her clothes off.

"Listen," I said. "For reasons I won't explain right now, I can't."

"What? Get out of the car."

"Goodnight, Taylor."

I stomped the gas and fled.

Like a coward.

Like a man broken.

30

The phone woke me. I sat up stupidly in the sea of white sheets, searched for the source of the ringing, and located my cell after nine years.

"Hello," I mumbled.

"Not at church?"

"I don't go."

"I recommend Olive Branch Baptist," the voice said.

"Andrews," I said, identifying the voice.

"Yeah?"

"Detective Andrews. Just figured out who you are," I said.

"Late night?"

"What do you want."

"To update you. On Murphy and his friendly neighborhood drug distribution service. He didn't exactly have a marijuana wholesale warehouse, but we found enough."

"Good."

"We don't think he's very well connected, and it doesn't appear he knows much about the murder of Mackenzie Allen."

"I got that impression too. Who supplies him?"

"This is tobacco county, August. Thousands of acres full of

tobacco leaves. People pay their bills by growing tobacco, and buy new trucks by growing weed here and there. Impossible to bust them all. Murphy had twenty sources, at least."

"So you bagged a dealer," I said. "But that's it."

"Exactly. We're stone cold on the murder. We dragged in the usual troublemakers, a few informants, and nothing. Nobody knows anything, nobody has heard anything. We're not even sure which direction to look."

"Same here," I said and rubbed my eyes.

"The paper is roasting us," he said. For the first time since I met him, he sounded frustrated. "Same story, front page, every day. And we've still got nothing." I smiled and remembered the intense pressure from the LA media. I didn't miss that. "You've done a lotta homicide investigations, right?"

"Lotta people die in Los Angeles. The City of Angels. And homicides."

"You have me there. I only do a small handful per year. Is this normal? No leads, nothing suspicious, nobody knows anything?"

"Nope. This is bizarre. Either that or you suck at your job."

"Come in soon. We'll compare clues."

"You have clues?"

I hung up and stared at the ceiling, picturing the note I had received on my keyboard. A lot of questions would be answered if I could solve that card. Each day I woke wondering if a new note was waiting for me.

I stared at the far wall and last night's events played across it like a movie screen. We'd driven frantically back to her place, her mouth and hands everywhere. Old emotions slammed into me. Old and new. Taylor laughing and teasing, her fantastic sexy smile. If I'd stayed, the next hour or two would've been marvelous and hot and steamy, and I wanted it. I hadn't had a night like that in a while.

But I'd moved to South Hill to get away from things like that. Empty things. Things that hurt the next morning. Taylor would be a drug and leave me flying high just to crash in a few hours, depressed and miserable.

I pictured her. The blue shirt in her fists, a slow sultry look on her face. The ripples of her abdomen, the soft mounds over her lacy bra, toned shoulders, moonlight...

"Scrambled eggs and sausage." My father walked in holding a plate and a glass of orange juice. "You'll need to get your strength back, after last night."

31

That night my father put Kix to bed and we played a quick game of Backgammon, and then he left for Roanoke. Like most nights, I spent thirty minutes cleaning up blankets, books and toys from the floor. He hadn't learned to crawl so the mess remained centralized. I was getting pretty tired of washing his high chair tray and his bottles. Lucky he's worth it. Then I sat down with popcorn to watch football. Sunday night is football night.

As I watched, I thought about my father. A good man but he had changed, getting lost after Mom died. He dated a lot, and had received messages from several women during our weekend. Lost within work, within accomplishments, retirement property, women, gadgets, and more women. But he still walked around like most of the world, hoping no one would notice how lonely he was.

My phone rang.

"Hey Mack," Mr. Cannon said. Mr. Cannon was the long-haired, skinny, nosey computer whiz who taught seventh-grade English.

"Hey Mr. Cannon."

"You know, you can call me Trevor."

"Hey Trevor."

"Hey, I was just calling to let you know," he said, "about our

Wednesday night service this week. Our Wednesday night services are real nice. Real good time. This Wednesday we're cooking Brunswick stew."

"How was church today?" I asked. This was the third call I'd gotten from him in a month. He went to church, brought home the bulletin and let me know about all the upcoming dates. He won the honor of being my most persistent friend.

"Real nice. Pastor shared about apple pie and how it can't be apple pie without apples. And we're the same way, except with the Bible."

"I don't have a clue what that means, Cannon."

"Anyway, let me know if you want to go. Brunswick stew is real good."

We hung up, and I munched on popcorn and thought about stew. Maybe I'd go.

My phone rang again.

"Hi, is this Mack?"

"The one and only."

"Hey Mack, it's Sam. From yesterday."

"Sam," I said slowly. Carla's husband. "From yesterday. No bells. Sorry."

"I'm really funny," he said. "Remember?"

"How'd you get my number?"

"South Hill Middle staff directory. Online. I'm sorry to bother you so late."

"No problem. What's up."

"I, jeez," he said. "I don't really know how to say this, or why I'm calling. I suppose just to warn you. Though I imagine you don't need it."

"Probably not. I'm very strong. Warn me of?"

"Aaron and Roy, mostly," he said.

"Oh no. They have guns and beards and everything."

"Can we keep this phone call between us?"

"Probably," I said.

"Okay. They both got their pot from Jon," he said. "And you were recently reported to have busted Jon. Not a lot of potheads around here love you right now."

"That's a shame. They're such a highly sought after demographic."

"Roy spent the night in jail for drunk driving last night too. His wife called us, furious. They think you tipped the cops."

"Gasp," I said.

"Yeah. Those two guys usually find a way to run off whoever Taylor brings around. I think it's some game they play. She does it on purpose."

"You're a good guy, Sam. I appreciate the warning."

"No problem, Mack."

"Did you know Mackenzie Allen?"

"Yeah, a little. Played cards with him once."

"Lots of card players in South Hill," I said.

"There's not a lot else to do."

"Where does everyone play?"

"Different places. Jon Murphy's, quite a bit."

"Think he'll invite me to the next one?" I asked. He laughed. I'm a riot. Back on top. "Did Aaron know Mackenzie Allen?"

"Yeah. Aaron and Roy both knew Mackenzie Allen, but never liked him much."

"Why not?"

"Because of Taylor. Taylor has a guy to flirt with wherever she goes. She visits a lot of hunt clubs. The one you saw yesterday is a piece of crap. There are some really nice ones. TV, satellite, air-conditioning, refrigerators, everything. She has a guy she's stringing along at each club. Sorry to be the one telling you all this. But she used to flirt with Mackenzie Allen at school, and not with Roy. Made Roy mad."

"Roy hated Mackenzie Allen," I said. "And now Mackenzie Allen's dead."

"Yeah," he said. "But I'm sure Roy didn't do it."

"Did Taylor ever date Deputy Andrews? Captain America-looking guy?"

"Yeah. Yeah, she did. You know him?"

"Not really," I said.

"He's one of the many."

"Sounds like you're not thrilled with your wife's friend selection."

"Well," he chuckled into the phone. "I really like Taylor. And only partially because she was the hottest girl in South Hill. Other than Carla, of course."

"Course."

"She's got a lot going on for her. Including men issues, unfortunately."

"Actually," I said. "I think her taste has improved recently."

"Yeah," he said and I could tell he was smiling. "But not by much."

32

I knocked on Taylor's door and walked into her classroom during our planning period. She sat reclined in her chair, facing the door. Her right leg was crossed over her left and she bounced her right shoe, a red kitten-heeled sandal, on the end of her toes. Her left sandal lay on the floor beside her foot. Toenails painted a dark wine color. I couldn't see the color of her skirt, it was so short. Her blouse was a tight, pale white.

"Well, well. Changed your mind, preacher man? Come to eat the forbidden fruit?"

"Look at that. A biblical allusion."

"I'm a christian too, you know," she said.

"Tell you the truth, I'm not sure what that means. I thought I once did, but I think maybe it's a subjective thing. Like saying you're rich, but by whose standards?"

"What's your definition of a christian?" she asked.

"I don't know. What's yours?"

"I don't know either," she said. "How can you be terrible at this? You're a preacher."

"I used to work at a church, with their youth group. I'm not a preacher."

"I don't know." She shrugged. "I go to church."

"I don't anymore."

"Then you aren't a christian."

"I think that just means I'm not on an attendance roll some-where," I said. "And I shouldn't have kissed you."

"The hell you shouldn't," she said. "You shouldn't have stopped. You shouldn't have dropped me off and left."

"You and I are after two different things."

"I'm just after some fun, preacher man. Especially with you."

"And I'm doing my best to avoid exactly that."

That stopped her. Her leg quit bouncing.

"Why?"

"I've had that kind of fun for almost a decade. Made me miserable and mean. Now, I'm waiting. For something substantive."

"And I'm not it," she snapped.

"You're probably somebody's real thing. But not mine. We don't fit."

"The kissing fit."

"The kissing..." Was out of this world. "Was a mistake. No matter how it felt."

"Are you a queer preacher?"

She stood and walked barefoot to stand in front of me. Her body stood so close to mine she had to look all the way up to see me. I started to feel overheated. And prurient.

"I know you're not queer," she said. "Because I can tell you want me."

"Never said I didn't. Just can't."

"You're not impotent. I can tell that too."

"I have to go grade papers," I said.

"Wuss."

MY PLANNING PERIOD seemed to last forever. I sat staring at my door, hoping Taylor wouldn't walk in. She had already sent me an email. It said, *How long do you think you can run from me*? I wasn't sure if I could turn her down again. Walking out of her classroom and driving away from her place had been some of the toughest decisions of my life. Giving in would have been easy. And so fun. So much fun. I hurt thinking about it.

My door opened. My heart stopped.

"So," Kristen said. She was the blonde teacher from Radford, married to Curtis. "I'm impressed."

"With?"

"You." She walked in and sat in a chair near me. She wore comfortable black shoes, black slacks and a gray shirt. "I didn't think any man would be able to turn her down. I'm not even sure if my husband could."

"Yes he could. You're worth it."

"Thanks. Still, I'm impressed."

"Don't be. If it'd been her instead of you just now, I might have caved."

"You really are a good man, aren't you?" she said.

"I'm a desperate man. Desperate to do things right."

"You decided not to roll in the hay with Taylor Williams because you don't think you two will end up together. That's something a good man would do."

"You found out about this quick."

"I'm a girl. She's a girl. She needed someone to cry to."

"She cried?" I asked.

"Not bawling. But yeah, a little."

"Wow," I said. "Probably because I'm handsome, huh."

"Probably because you're a pig."

"I'm joking. Making jokes helps you ignore things, like pain, you know."

"Is that why you're always making lame jokes?"

I frowned. That showed her.

"What kind of right things are you trying to do?" she asked.

That question was too big to answer. Too big of a concept, too big of a change in my life. There was no easy way to express my former despair compared to current hope.

"She's a cistern," I said.

"A what?"

"A leaky cistern."

"Oh."

"It's a metaphor," I said wisely.

"I'm aware. Still don't get it."

"Water was precious in the ancient Middle East, and so they'd keep it in cisterns, underground holding tanks. You'd survive if your cistern was holding water," I said. "We all keep our life in different cisterns, hoping they'll hold, support us, keep us alive. Family, job, alcohol, whatever. Some cisterns are healthy, some aren't. One of mine used to be having fun with girls. Girls like her. They were a cistern for me, where I put a lot of energy, time, and self-worth. Except it didn't hold water. Doesn't work. Never fills. Leaves you empty inside."

"I get it."

"But you don't," I said. "You wouldn't get it unless you've been exhausted pouring yourself into relationships and gratification only to realize it's shallow and empty. Work so hard and end up even lonelier. It's a scary feeling."

"I can tell."

"Fun isn't the goal. Fun leaks," I said.

"Wow." She smiled. A great, big beautiful smile. "You hate talking about yourself. This is an encouraging change."

"There are things worth talking about."

"How do you know Taylor's not the girl?"

"I figure the right girl won't show up at my door in heels with wine the first week I meet her."

"You're kidding!"

"Don't act surprised. I'm handsome."

"That's like a pornographic movie," she said.

"You shouldn't watch porn."

"I don't. I was playing off a stereotype."

"I wouldn't know."

"Uh huh," she said.

"But you're right. That first night, she might as well have worn a sign that read, 'Not right for you.'"

"Probably wouldn't have matched the heels," she reasoned.

"Plus, I think the only reason she wants to date me is because I'm the only one in South Hill she hasn't."

I JAMMED my small gardening hand shovel into the ground and wiped my forehead.

"Gardening is not for sissies," I said. The autumn sun had increased its intensity when it saw me gardening, or so it felt.

"You noticed," Ms. Allen said.

Kix and I'd brought Ms. Allen a tray of burgundy fall chrysanthemums. We caught her gardening, as I'd hoped we would. As soon as Kix saw her he'd held out his arms and she hadn't let go since.

I had six of the dozen flowers planted in front of the house, in the partial shade of the porch. Behind me in a pile lay the tulip bulbs that hadn't flowered well earlier in the year. I'd been instructed to pull them out and replace them. The six planted flowers were packed in with soil so I redistributed the mulch and started on a new location with the seventh.

"Oh, Mack, he's just the cutest boy."

"He prefers sexy and capable," I said.

"So cute." She nuzzled Kix's cheek and he smiled and patted her nose.

"I hate weeds," I said, and pulled out another handful for the growing collection behind me. "I read once a weed is but an unloved flower. But I disagree. Weeds are stupid."

"Impressive, aren't they."

"They don't look like much, but they're everywhere."

"Everywhere there's no healthy growth."

"There's a healthy analogy in there somewhere, but I'm too sweaty to find it."

"So what brings you to visit me, Mack?" she said. She tipped up a glass of lemonade to Kix's lips. He gaped like a fish and managed to swallow some. If videos of Ms. Allen feeding a toddler lemonade surfaced on Facebook, protective moms everywhere would call for her excommunication.

"I read," I said, and piled topsoil around roots of the eighth and ninth chrysanthemums, "somewhere, that true religion is taking care of orphans and widows. I don't know how to do that. But I noticed you like gardening and then I noticed these flowers."

"You're a good kid, Mackenzie," she said. "We widows need all the help we can get. How is the investigation coming?"

"I can't speak for the police, but I'm annoying people and hoping something will turn up."

"Is that official procedure?"

"No. But I'm not official."

"Can I pay you?"

"I'm also not a mercenary."

"Private detectives aren't mercenaries. Are they?"

"Being a PI is their job. It's not mine. I'm just your friendly, neighborhood middle school teacher," I said.

"Not many middle school teachers have muscles like yours."

"Or hearts of gold like mine."

Kix pointed at the lemonade and grunted. I was quickly forgotten as Kix got all the lemonade he wanted and then got a tour of the front yard. I planted the rest of the flowers, finished spreading the mulch, threw the weeds into her trash can, filled up her watering can and soaked the ground around the fall flowers. After taking off an old pair of gloves that had belonged to her late husband, I drained my lemonade.

"What else?" I asked.

"Would you mind changing a few lightbulbs?"

"Not at all."

I balanced on chairs and replaced a few old bulbs with the funny-looking energy-saving ones. Kix and Debbie Allen looked at pictures around the house. Kix was a good audience. As I stepped down from the last bulb I noticed an ascending group of framed wall photographs, chronicling Mackenzie Allen's school pictures up through twelfth grade. I could feel the house's recent and sudden emptiness and loneliness like a raw wound, made all the more sad by the framed glossy smiles. He favored his father, judging by a picture of both the Allen men holding up fish for the camera.

"Okay. I release you. You may go."

She walked to the car holding Kix and buckled him in before kissing me on the cheek.

"I appreciate the visit very much, Mr. August. Please come again soon."

"You got it."

33

I stood beside the green of the fourth hole. From there, I watched golfers approach and putt, and then tee off on hole five. A generous opposing coach had suggested it during our first match in September. I also bought a visor similar to the one he wore during that first match. Standing beside the fourth green, with my visor and sunglasses, I was a seasoned veteran.

South Hill Middle had this match with Bluestone Middle rescheduled due to the murder earlier in the month. Otherwise, golf season would already be over. Today marked the final day of golf. Our team wasn't in contention for postseason play. We stunk.

Attendance at golf matches also stunk. A very small handful of faithful parents showed, and today so did Mr. Cummings.

Mr. Cummings was on the school board. I'd seen him once touring the middle school. He had silver gray hair combed to the side and had I been a fifty-year-old lady I'd probably swoon. Today he wore a dark green suit, with an even darker green, expensive tie with a gold tie-bar and gold cufflinks. On his right hand gleamed a large gold ring. Looked like a Virginia Tech ring. Money personified.

"Mr. August." He had an easy, practiced smile. I wanted to buy something from him already. He held out his hand sideways, palm up. I considered giving him five, but shook his hand instead. "I'm Russ Cummings, of Cummings Financial Planning. Hell of a team you got here."

"I see you haven't been checking the scorecards, Mr. Cummings."

"Hah," he chuckled and clapped me on the shoulder. "I'm not talking about the score, Mr. August. I'm talking about the boys. Fine young men."

"That they are."

"You've done a good job here. Helluva job. We're very proud of you. I'm on the school board, I guess I should have mentioned that."

"The school board is proud of South Hill Middle's golf team?" I asked.

"We're proud of all our teams, Mr. August. And especially our coaches. We know a good thing when we see it."

Flattery never appealed to me, especially when it smelled of bull, so I said nothing. One of our golfers bounced a ball onto the lip of the green from one hundred fifty yards out. I clapped, but not as loudly as Mr. Cummings. He also whistled.

"Beautiful day," he said. He clasped his hands behind his back and looked around at the trees, which looked more and more like fireworks as the days advanced into fall. Autumn in the flat tobacco lands of southern VA was going to be spectacular. LA might have great weather year round, but it didn't have this. "Perfect day for golf."

"Most days are."

"Maybe I'll take you golfing one day. My treat. Before the weather turns cold. What do you say to that?"

"I'd say I'm sure glad I wore my lucky underwear. Good stuff always happens to me when I wear them."

He took his time before answering.

"You're making sport of me, aren't you?"

"Just killing time until you get to the good stuff."

"How do you know there is good stuff?" he asked. He'd mustered up his smile again.

"This is the first match you've been to. You're proud of me. And you won't look at me."

"That's right," he said slowly as if remembering something. He shook a finger at me. "You are used to interrogating people. I'm not going to slip much by you, huh?"

"Especially not a triple homicide, so don't try."

"An honest, straightforward man," he said, and pounded me on the back of my shoulder again. "I like that."

"I try."

"I spoke recently with Sheriff Mitchell."

"Mkay."

"He said the investigation isn't going very well. But he did say that you've been a big boon to the department. Your cooperation has benefited them a great deal."

"Sheriff Mitchell. That sweet talker." He was lying. The sheriff would never use the word boon or call my cooperation a benefit.

"In fact, he told me you're looking for the killer yourself."

Two golfers walked by and I looked at Stephen's scorecard.

"Not bad, Stephen," I said. I nodded at the golfer from Bluestone that he was paired with. "How is he playing?"

"Good. But I think I'm beating him."

"You're doing great. Keep up the good work. Proud of you. Stay loose. Remember, you make better contact if you're not tense. Swing fast, not hard."

"Thanks, Coach." Stephen and the other golfer walked to the next tee box.

"You're a natural," Mr. Cummings said.

"I try. It's fun."

"Mackenzie Allen's murder was a terrible tragedy and we all hope his murderer is brought to justice. We offer all the support to the sheriff's department we can."

I nodded, watching the next pair of golfers line up approach shots.

"I'd like to take you into my confidence, Mr. August," he said, still sounding like a politician.

"Sure."

"Can you guarantee that this conversation will be kept between us?"

"Nope."

That startled him.

"I would like to share with you an inside perspective that the school board has, Mr. August, but it has to stay between us."

"No promises, Mr. Cummings. I'm a man of integrity, and I don't gossip. But if your dirty little secret needs to be brought into the light, I might be the one to drag it there."

"I do not have dirty secrets."

"I doubt that. But if so, then you've nothing to fear," I said.

He watched the golfers with his hands in his pockets. Frustration was evident on his face.

"I shall trust your discretion, young man. You may or may not be aware that our school system is in the unfortunate position of having a terrible superintendent. Man by the name of Louis Neal. His judgment is unsound, his decisions are rash, and he does not have the proper respect for the school board that he ought. The school board members are officials elected by the public to properly oversee the schools. And our superintendent behaves like a selfish tyrant. I imagine your fellow teachers have all been saying the same things. Have they not?"

"I'm not much of a gossip, Mr. Cummings." I smiled. One of my good ones.

"Regardless. Something must be done about the superintendent. And while," he said slowly, and licked his lips before continuing. "And while Mackenzie Allen's murder was very sad and awful, it does have the silver lining of throwing Neal's leadership into question. A teacher was killed at a local school over which he is the superintendent, and nothing has been done about the murder. He sits there and does nothing. Not a damn thing."

"Think he should be out there with a flashlight and magnifying glass, looking for clues?"

"The school board is going to call for his resignation next week. That must stay between us, Mr. August. Absolutely must. Many problems will be solved with him gone. And the ongoing murder investigation is the convenient solution."

"Ah."

"Surely you've seen this done in politics before, Mr. August."

"Surely."

"The public wants action, demands justice. Someone must pay."

"You don't think it should be the killer?" I asked, but he didn't pay attention. He was deep into his rehearsed speech.

"Someone must be held accountable for the murder, which should have been prevented. Often in politics, someone innocent is sacrificed to appease the public. But in our case, happily we can sacrifice someone guilty. Louis Neal. Not necessarily guilty of the murder, but of other atrocities."

"That bastard."

"It will satisfy the public, convince them that the schools are in good hands, show them that action is being taken to keep the children safe.

"Now this, Mr. August, is what I truly wish to share with you. All of us on the school board want the killer brought to justice. We all are deeply committed to that. However, it would benefit us if that...didn't happen within the next couple weeks."

"So that the superintendent would still look weak and responsible for the murder when you fire him," I said.

"Yes."

"You want the murderer caught, but after the superintendent is gone."

"Precisely. Allow some good to come from Mr. Allen's death. I know it's a bit unorthodox, but what do you think?"

"I think that if you and Mr. Neal are enemies, then I'm probably on his side."

34

Mr. Charlie's lunch period was the same as mine. I knew this because I peeked at his schedule when the secretary was signing in a few packages from the delivery guy. However, he never ate in the cafeteria. I buzzed his room over the intercom.

"Yes?" he said.

"Mr. Charlie, this is Mr. August. You eating in your room today?"

"Yessir, I am."

"I'm going to join you."

"Why, that sounds great," he said, and I hung up.

The art teacher ate in his large, airy classroom because he painted while he lunched. I sat down with my turkey sandwich and watched him work for a few minutes. He'd taken off his "Jesus" tie to paint. He slowly and quietly explained why he tended to paint impressionistic artwork, why he always kept a small color pallet, painted the furthest objects first, darker paint on the canvas before light, thinner paint sticking to heavier, techniques of brush strokes. I soon forgot my lunch and watched an evergreen tree line take shape beneath a mountain.

"I bet, Mr. August, that you ain't come to watch me paint."

"I came to talk about our school board," I said, snapping back to reality. "Don't know much about it, and you're the first I ever heard mention it."

"Last month," he said. "Before Mackenzie Allen died." His face was close to the canvas and he spoke out of the corner of his mouth, like the muscles in his face were paralyzed with concentration.

"Bingo."

"You've come to the right place, Mr. August. I worked here twelve years, I drive the school buses, I preach in the churches, and I live near the school board office. I attend the meetings regularly."

"So. Is Louis Neal a doofus?"

His brush left the canvas and he turned to face me. Flecks of paint dotted his skin.

"That's a nasty thing for a preacher to say."

"I'm not a preacher. I heard someone say it."

"You sound like one of the school board," he scoffed and returned to work. "No, Mr. Neal is no doofus. I like him, respect him, and so do most people who attend the meetings. And the board of supervisors, they like him because he's financially efficient."

"Just so I'm not getting my boards mixed up, the board of supervisors is in charge of the whole county, including the school board, which is specifically in charge of the county schools. Correct?"

"Correct."

"So why does the School Board dislike him?"

He chuckled and shook his head. "Everyone got their theories, Mr. August. I got mine."

"What's yours."

"Well," he said, turned, and exchanged his brush for his sandwich. "You can't repeat this."

"Sure. I came to you. Lips are sealed."

"Lotta of people share my opinion, I think. But I heard a rumor someone got fired for voicing them. I think the school board don't like Mr. Neal because three of the board members have spouses who work at Gaston Elementary. Have you heard of Gaston Elementary, Mr. August?"

"No."

He took a bite of his sandwich, and chewed as slowly as he talked, before continuing.

"Gaston Elementary is in the southern part of the county. The school is tiny. It's only got fifty kids enrolled."

"Wow. That's not very many," I said. I had no idea if that was a lot for an elementary school or not. But I'm helpful.

"Exactly. So, Mr. Neal wants to close the school and have other elementary schools absorb the students. Gaston Elementary keeps on custodians, kitchen staff, principals, all the usual staff a school has, guys like me, but only for fifty kids. The money being spent per kid at that school? Really high. Close to double other elementary schools."

"Crazy," I encouraged.

"Yeah, it really is crazy, Mr. August. Which is why the superintendent wants to shut it down. It'd save the county several hundred thousand dollars."

"But," I said. "Several school board members have spouses who work there."

"Right. They can't come out and say it, of course, but everyone knows the real reason that school is still open. And the raises, too. You heard about those?"

"Consider me uninformed."

"Teachers in Mecklenburg County have been getting tiny raises for years. Disrespectful, you ask me. I been here for twelve, and I bet I'm not making much more than you. The superintendent, he been making the case that the raises could be more substantial if Gaston Elementary is closed because the county would have an extra half million to spend."

"Sounds like a good idea to me."

"All teachers think so. Me included. So, Mecklenburg's board of supervisors increases the Public Schools' budget last year, and the School Board decides to use the money to only significantly raise the salary of two groups of employees. The administrators and the guidance counselors. Just to stick it to the board of supervisors, you understand me. And wouldn't you know it, one member of the school board has a husband who's the assistant principal at Blue Stone Elementary, and one member has a wife who's a guidance counselor at South Hill High. Mr. Neal was so mad he went to the press about it."

I whistled. I'd seen that happen before, and I'd seen it backfire. If you throw inside, you might end up hitting the batter. I love baseball analogies.

"Yeah, exactly. That's why I asked you if you been reading about all the turmoil. You were hired when all of this started blowing up, Mr. August. The board yells at each other, because a couple of them don't agree with the decisions, but they're outvoted. Five to two. The board, they yell at Neal and he yells back. The board been yelling at teachers who attend and complain. They try to stop the newspaper stringer from attending, but the sheriff intervened and let him stay."

We sat chewing for a few minutes.

"Seems to me," I said. "Based on your account, that the school board is going to a lot of trouble for a couple jobs. Their spouses could get jobs at other schools. They're married to School Board members. What else do you need to get a job as a teacher? Why all the fighting."

"You think that way," he smiled. "Because you ain't from this area. The more you see of the world, the less significant small parts of it become. I ain't from here either. But a lot of people never leave South Hill. Including some school board members. They were born here, their parents taught at Gaston Elementary, they went to school here, they don't go far for college and then they came straight back. Closing Gaston Elementary ain't completely about the money. It's also about who's in control. The school board members, who lived here their whole lives? Or the superintendent, who moved here when he got hired."

"How dare he come here and try to close one of the schools," I said.

"That's exactly what the school board thinks, Mr. August. It's about money. But it's also about control, and the way things ought to be, and the way things have always been. It's about a way of life. It's their history, a part of who they are."

"Mr. Charlie, I think you're more insightful than you let on."

"Naw, not me. I teach art and drive buses and preach. I don't get all riled. Can't understand the anger. But there is, you know. They get so mad. Mad enough to be separated by deputies a couple of times."

"That's pretty mad."

ON THE WAY HOME, I rolled the windows down and blared The Killers. Kix loved it when the windows dropped, and he grinned and fought the invisible rush of air until my phone rang.

"August," I said.

"Bingham. Your favorite Los Angeles police sergeant. Whatever happened with that note?"

"The note from the killer? I don't like thinking about it," I said, and buzzed up the front windows. "Because then I remember I know nothing."

"Rookie mistake. You're an old pro making a rookie mistake."

"The note could be anything. I don't know what to do about it other than show it around and ask people if they wrote it."

"So what? That always works," he said.

"Shouldn't you be arresting someone? Crime take a holiday in LA?"

"You got it. All the whites and blacks and Latinos are holding hands and singing in the parking lot. Do what you can about that note. That thing makes me nervous."

"What about school boards? They make you nervous?" I asked.

"School Boards, hell yeah they do. Big power grab, getting yourself elected onto a school board."

"Seen any violence come out of one?"

"Especially in tougher school districts. Those boards influence big decisions, like personnel, busing students in and out of nice schools, sports."

"What do you mean sports?"

"The athletic directors work with the school boards sometimes to negotiate with other counties. I'd think in a small town the football and basketball rival games would be about as big as it gets."

"How do you know so much about school boards?"

"I'm old and wise. Plus, I had an uncle on a School Board. Only lasted one term, he hated it."

"You're old? Forty is old now?"

"Thirty-nine, jackass," he said, and he hung up.

35

Mackenzie August had his ducks in a row, yessir.

My electric bill was paid. I kept the AC off and the windows open to reduce the cost. My cable bill was paid. I canceled the movie channels. Life's too short. My gas bill and water bill were paid. My credit card balance had shrunk two months in a row. Next month I was going to have enough left over money to pay off an old medical bill. I drank more water and ate more fruit these days. I slept better.

Now if I could only quit making out with other teachers. Taylor had begun sending me inappropriate selfies, and they weakened my willpower. To occupy my mind I played online poker. And drank. And cursed when I lost.

Mackenzie August. Work in progress.

I threw the laptop onto the couch beside me. The house was quiet and cool. It was always quiet and cool, after my little monster went to bed. Night after night. For almost two months. I needed a hobby, otherwise I'd go crazy before Christmas. Maybe I should watch TV and play video games every night. I craved competition. Of any kind. Even competition of the mind. Like poker. Maybe I should play another game of poker. Good idea.

First, I checked on Kix. Super Dad. He was asleep on the far end of the crib, on top of both his covers and his bear. Like most nights, I ended up sitting on the edge of the bed and watching him breathe. Some nights I slept here. When I did, I had fewer nightmares.

I thought about murderers less while I watched him. I didn't worry about Resource Officer Reed coming to throw rocks at my door at two in the morning, or about Jon Murphy seeking revenge with a bunch of drugged-out buddies. Taylor couldn't reach me when I was in Kix's room.

But I couldn't stay there. I had a poker game to play. I sat back down in my La-Z-Boy and thought about Taylor and her legs. Then I pondered Roy and Roy's temper and again talked myself out of believing he had anything to do with Mackenzie Allen's death. Roy was mean and had access to guns, but he didn't register as a killer to my highly fallible killer radar. Nor could I picture him using a .22. Too proud. However, if I believed that, I was left again with no leads.

Other than the school board. My conversation with Mr. Charlie had been eye-opening. After our tête-à-tête I'd done some research. Some of the richest and most powerful people in the county sat on the school board. That hadn't taken long to discover. In fact, the collective wealth and influence sitting on the school board appeared to be significantly superior to the district members sitting on the board of supervisors. That fact had to gall both boards. I didn't understand why prosperous and busy people sacrificed their time to sit on the school board and yell at each other. But I wasn't from around heah.

That's how people from South Hill pronounced "here." Heah. I liked it.

I'd read through copies of recent newspapers; the superintendent, the school board, the board of supervisors, the irate teachers and the irate parents were making the front page every few days. The reporters from the paper didn't do a great job at hiding their opinions: the school board members were bad people. Especially my favorite, Mr. Cummings. He and the majority of the school board seemed to be furious in most articles. They were furious with the superintendent and looking for a way to sack him. They were furious with teachers, and wished they'd shut up. Furious with the board of supervisors and with each other. Furious enough to require deputy sheriffs' intervention on more than one occasion.

I'd seen similar wars within LA gangs. What appeared insignificant to outsiders was huge to the powerful and proud members of gangs. Small things became worth killing over, because small things were their life. In fact, considering how unimportant and insignificant the cause of gang violence often was, the school board rage became almost understandable. A hit ordered by a territorial, proud, rich business proprietor on the school board who'd attended Gaston Elementary as a youngster and whose wife still worked there became reasonable. Almost.

Three problems, though. One, did the whole school board order the hit? Probably not. So which one? Mr. Cummings? He's the only one I knew. Pretty amateurish reasoning. Two, individually or corporately, the school board members were weak suspects. I mostly considered them because I had no better suspect. That would change, however, if I could find a money trail. The love of money is the root of all kinds of nasty stuff. If you have five thousand dollars then you can get someone killed, but the risk was enormous. Not worth a few teacher salaries. But there could always be more cash hidden beneath the surface. The cash wouldn't, however, explain the note left for me by the killer.

The third problem was my biggest. Even if I felt really strongly about the school board suspect, or any other suspect for that matter, where did that leave me? I didn't have a badge. I couldn't haul them in, couldn't interrogate them. I couldn't go bother them at work, I had my own job. I had never investigated without a legal mandate, without a car and gun provided by the state for only one reason. I didn't know how to proceed. That thought left me frustrated and tired. Too tired for poker. I went to bed.

The last thing I thought about before falling asleep remained the same as previous nights: a killer still stalked South Hill. I could imagine him walking my lawn. The note lay in a drawer inside my classroom, but I carried the weight of it with me. The killer was interested in me and I was easy to find. On nights like tonight, Mackenzie Allen's murderer always stood right outside my window.

36

T he bell at South Hill Middle rang at 3:25 to end the day. The students, who are useless beginning at 3:20, had piled at the door and filtered out. The room went silent.

I spent thirty minutes grading papers. Math teachers have it easy. Students either get the right answer or they don't. English teachers have to decipher pages of handwriting. I bet English teachers buy more aspirin than math teachers.

A knock at the door, and Mackenzie Allen's mother walked in. This was the first time I'd seen her professionally dressed. She was a short woman, probably not five and half, and her hair was rich brown with silver streaks. She wore a dark khaki skirt suit that came to her knees. The collar was a cream color that matched her heels and her shoulder bag. She was attractive in a natural earthy sort of way.

"Mr. August." She smiled.

"You teach in that?" I stood from my desk.

"No. But thanks for noticing."

"My pleasure," I said, and we shook hands.

"Can we talk?"

"Certainly. Unless you're a reporter in disguise."

"I'm not. That's an odd qualifier."

"I'm an odd guy."

We sat down at the long worktable. She set her bag on the table and crossed her legs.

"I read through a few old newspapers to catch up on the world. I read about you," she said.

"Which occasion did you read about?"

"The drug raid."

"Ah. You can't prove that was me," I said. "The paper reported that *allegedly* the teacher who found your son's body also helped the police during the raid."

"So. Was it you?"

"Allegedly," I said.

"Are you afraid of repercussions from the...underbelly of South Hill?"

"No. Maybe a little. Mostly, though, I'm tired of students asking questions during class."

"You don't look like a man afraid of repercussions," she said.

"I bruise easily."

She laughed.

Still got it.

"How you holding up?" I asked.

Her face clouded and she said, "Okay. I'd be better if Mackenzie's killer was behind bars. Is the investigation at a standstill?"

I drummed my fingers on the table between us and thought about how much to share. No one on the East Coast knew about the mysterious note on my keyboard. That would need to change soon, however, but not necessarily with Ms. Allen. I decided to stay with safer topics.

"Did you recognize the drug dealer you read about?"

"Yes," she said. "Unfortunately. Jon Murphy. Mackenzie was friends with him. Was Mackenzie still into pot?"

"You knew?"

"I knew he used to. Caught him with it in high school. He and Jon

Murphy were in different grades but they both went to Blue Stone High. I've never trusted Jon."

"I think Mackenzie Allen smoked socially. Not much. Did you tell the sheriff that?"

"No," she said and shifted uncomfortably in her seat.

"What else can you tell me that you didn't tell the sheriff? It could help."

She leaned forward and rested her forehead on the heels of her hands, elbows sitting on the table.

"I don't know," she sighed. "I felt like I told them everything. I guess not."

"Did Mackenzie ever go places that he wouldn't talk about? Friends he wouldn't discuss?"

She shook her head without removing it from her hands. "No."

"He came up really clean. Nothing suspicious or strange other than drugs, which I'm pretty sure had nothing to do with his death. So I'm left with chasing down small leads. Anything small could be significant."

She nodded.

"What about Roy? Do you know Roy?"

"I know of him, yes. He teaches here, grew up in the county. Mackenzie mentioned him a couple times."

"What'd he say about him?"

"That they both liked the same girl, even though Roy was married. However, I heard, Mr. August, that you ended up with that girl." She raised up to look at me.

"Been listening to gossip?"

"Have you been kissing a girl at Kahills?"

"Allegedly."

"So it's true. I bet she fell for your Cajun accent."

"It was a mistake. Won't happen again."

"Why did you ask about Roy? Is he a suspect?"

"I heard that he and Mackenzie didn't get along. That's it. I'm chasing rumors."

"It's not Roy," she said, and shook her head. "Even if it wasn't a friendly rivalry, they were only boys being boys. Even though one of them should be acting like a grown man with a wife."

"What could Mackenzie Allen have been doing at the school so late?" I asked.

She shook her head.

"I don't know. I never did."

"You never knew what he did at night?" I asked.

"He was a very independent boy. Man, I guess. He didn't offer up many details."

"What about the school board?"

"Ugh," she said. "What about it?"

"Did he have beef with the school board?"

"Of course. Don't we all? He was so mad after that meeting he could barely speak."

"He went to a meeting?"

"Oh yes," she said. "Don't you read the paper?"

"When was it?"

"A week or two before he died. That was probably the same meeting at which you were officially hired, incidentally. The school board has to vote on all new hires."

"What was he doing there?"

"He went to request funding for instruments, copyrights for sheet music, basically an increase in the music department's budget. He hates band boosters. He asked last year, too, but they turned him down. He and a few of the board members got into a fight this time."

"Yelling or fists?"

"Yelling." She smiled sadly. "He was never violent, but he always spoke his mind."

"Who was he yelling at?"

"I don't remember. When he loses his temper it doesn't matter. Anyone close enough. Is this important?"

"Maybe," I said. "He had a bad temper?"

"Very bad. From his father."

"So what's the connection between the school board blow up and him being at the middle school so late?" I said.

"Mr. Charlie might know. He usually goes too."

"Goes? Goes where?"

"To the school. For their work nights, whatever they do," she said.

"Work nights? I haven't heard this before."

"I don't know much about them. I assumed it was a school-wide thing. The school system is short on custodial staff, so I think every once in a while they get together, buy pizza, sodas, beer maybe, and clean and paint or whatever needs to be done."

"Does the sheriff or Andrews know about them?"

"I assume so," she said.

"Ah hah."

"Ah hah?"

"This could be a clue. How often would you say Mackenzie was at the school late?"

"Once a month. Maybe more. There's not much to do around here and schools are a big deal. Wait until the end-of-the-year eighth-grade graduation. It's an enormous event. So, improving the school with your friends begins to actually sound fun."

"Who goes to the work nights?" I asked.

"I'm not sure. Ask Mr. Charlie, he can tell you."

"I plan to."

I TOLD STEPHEN, the eighth-grader in my class and on my golf team, that I'd take him to dinner anywhere within thirty miles. Any restaurant he wanted. We ended up at McDonalds a few miles from the school on Main Street. High class. Kix, however, liked Stephen's selection. He's a sucker for fries.

"Mr. August, have you seen *Band of Brothers*?" He wore the same beat-up white sneakers, jeans and red T-shirt he wore almost every day.

"Even better. I read the book *and* saw the movies."

"I saw them on the History Channel. What'd you think of them?"

"Those movies will make a man out of you." I dunked a chicken nugget into the small, plastic barbecue cup. Eating chicken nuggets was not an arbitrary process. Generally McDonalds let me down and didn't provide me with an adequate supply of sauce. In other words, I didn't get quite the coverage I'd prefer; I had to eat the nugget in one bite, instead of two. Two is optimal.

Perhaps I should focus.

"What's that mean?" he asked.

"The book is real, you know. Those stories actually happened to actual people. You can learn about loyalty, bravery, honor, courage, discipline, friendship by reading them. Or watching them."

"Yeah," he said. He'd gotten a large-sized Big Mac combo and a milkshake, and had already gone through three napkins.

"Can we talk about your dad?"

"Sure," he said, and he took a hard pull on his milkshake straw.

"When did he die?"

"A year ago."

"Cancer?"

He nodded, and said, "The death disease. That's what kids on my bus called it."

"And then Mr. Allen died too."

He nodded again. Kix watched us, quietly grabbing handfuls of fries and getting most of them in his mouth. He also had finished half a nugget I'd given him, out of my benevolence.

"And you're only thirteen, right?"

He nodded and took a bite of his burger.

"That's some pretty rough cards for a kid your age to be dealt."

"And Mom works, like, every night. Sometimes I don't see her for days. She's gone when I get home some, and asleep when I go to school."

"Where's she work?"

"The Holiday Inn. I hate that place. We can't even stay there for free."

"So what do you do at home?"

He shrugged and said, "Play video games. Do homework. Watch

TV. My stupid sister won't let me use the computer, and I don't live near any of my friends."

We sat chewing for a while. I got us all refills, including Kix's milk, and when I sat back down I took a deep breath.

"A few years ago I lost my mom to cancer. That same year my fiancée died. And later, when I was a police officer, my partner died. So I know a little bit about what you're going through."

He nodded.

"It's important to talk about this stuff sometimes. Otherwise it sits inside and festers. Talking lets it out, lets off some steam, you know?"

"I talked with the guidance counselor some."

"How'd it go?"

He shrugged and said, "Okay. I guess. She was pretty busy."

"That year when my mom and fiancée died, I thought the world was going to end. I didn't know what to do. Didn't know who to talk to, what to say to people, how to sleep at night. All the girls in my life were gone. Kinda like how all the men in your life are gone."

"My grandpa lives in South Carolina. I see him some."

"Yeah?"

"Like for holidays."

"I still hurt when I think about my mom and my fiancée. Like you still hurt when you think about your dad and Mr. Allen. And it's going to hurt forever. But eventually it'll hurt much less and it'll be a part of who you are. The pain will be an important part of your past. But you're going to be okay. You know? You're a tough kid. Very smart. You are smart enough to earn scholarships to go to college, which is what you should be planning on."

"I think I want to be a Marine," he said.

"Very cool. That's a noble profession. That's why you liked *Band of Brothers.*"

"Yeah."

"It hurts. It always will. But you'll survive. You were made for a reason, and like Captain Winters from *Band of Brothers,* you've been wounded but you're still going and you can lead people one day. You're a tough guy, and I'll help. Okay?"

He nodded.

I popped a nugget. Captain Winters was the larger-than-life hero from Ambrose's story, and I knew I'd earned cool points for referencing him.

"Do you play Halo?" he asked me.

I smiled and breathed a sigh of relief. I think we had just bonded.

37

Faculty meetings take place once a month, and give the teachers an opportunity to revert back into students and force the principal to shush them like they shush students all day long. One of the administrators always brings cake or cookies that only the brave eat due to the lonely walk up to the dessert table, and the invisible but almost audible judgment that grows with each step. An agenda is handed out and the principal shouts through the bullets in between shushes. I hate faculty meetings.

I sat near the back near Mrs. Ballard and Ms. Friedmond, and glanced over the agenda. Item two was an update from our representative to the school board. I got out my pen. Constant vigilance!

"Hey stud," Taylor Williams said, and she slid next to me. I was forced to look around her to see the principal. I wondered if she waited until I sat down before choosing her seat. If so, it was a perfect blitz. "I dare you to kiss me."

"Double dare?"

"Triple dare," she said. She smiled and moved halfway toward me. I could feel the stares from the two women nearby.

"Ew gross. You're a girl and girls are gross, which is what a kid in my fifth period told me," I said, because I couldn't think of anything else. I'm so manly.

"Fine. How about footsie?" she asked, and so I kicked her. She squeaked and kicked me back. Fortunately Principal Martin began shushing us and I focused so intently on her I could almost count the threads in her jacket.

The first item of the day was a recognition of the upcoming November birthdays. Thankfully we didn't sing. I wondered if this could be attributed to past failures.

The principal obviously dreaded the school board discussion. I bet her desire to get it out of the way got it planted second on the agenda. She called on Mrs. Laken to give us the report, and she did so in a nonchalant manner but anyone watching could see her gearing up for a fight.

Mrs. Laken stood and read from her prepared notes. Her first note was that the school board and board of supervisors had approved the proposed traffic light near the school, but could not pay for it. The School, PTA, boosters, somebody else would have to provide the funds.

"Well how are we going to do that?" Ms. Ballard asked. She did not raise her hand and interrupted Mrs. Laken's rhythm. "We already have to pay for everything else."

"We're not sure," Principal Martin answered. "This was only recently decided, and Vice Principal Mr. Baskins and the budget committee will review our finances and see what they can come up with. They haven't had a chance to investigate this yet. Obviously we'd all prefer if they paid for it. Next item."

"But that stoplight is necessary for the safety of our buses," Ms. Ballard argued, alternating between glaring at Mrs. Laken and Ms. Martin and searching for sympathy among those seated around her. "I'm sorry but I think that's ridiculous. We shouldn't have to beg them for funds, when we just want to be safe."

"I appreciate your concern, Ms. Ballard. That's why you head up the Safety Committee. Next item."

"Next, the raise for this year was voted on for one percent."

Outrage. Pandemonium. Most of the more vocal staff began complaining and shouting immediately. Mrs. Laken glared and shouted back, yelling that it was not her decision and she was just as mad as them. Some of the ire was turned on the principal, who looked defensive and understanding and concerned and professional all at once while trying to calm the room. The quieter staff, like Mr. Cannon, soon got irritated with the louder staff and started sighing and asking them to let Mrs. Laken finish. I wondered if I could make it to the cake and back with no one noticing.

"This is such bullshit," Taylor said. "I don't get paid enough to deal with the little pricks' bull every day. What are you writing?"

I looked down and realized I had been jotting names of certain teachers I was watching and gauging reactions.

"Why'd you write Roy's name down?"

"Remind myself I want to borrow his rake."

"Don't ask. He hates you. I bet we could sneak out."

"And go where?" I asked. Dumb question. Like tossing up a softball.

"My room. My chair is padded. I could sit on your lap," she said and leaned sideways toward me and bobbed her eyebrows. Her light orange shirt wasn't exactly off the shoulder, but close. I could smell her shampoo. Her face was near mine, and she looked soft.

"And miss all the fun?"

"My room would be fun. I'd lock the door."

"Okay!" Ms. Martin shouted. "Okay, let's try to focus. Nobody, shhhh, please, nobody in this room had anything to do with that vote. It's no use getting mad at each other."

"You know what I think," said Mr. Alexander. He was an old, grizzled Special Ed. Teacher who spoke slowly and deliberately, prone to exaggeration and instigation. The quieter, proper teachers all groaned. "I'll tell you exactly what I think," he drawled. He spoke so loudly that we had no choice but to listen. "I think we don't get our raises because the school board wanted new chairs to sit in twice a month, and new tables."

"And raises for themselves!"

A whole new batch of arguments broke out. Taylor took my pen and began drawing on my paper. I expected when she finished it would be a dirty cartoon.

"We're not going to talk about this any further!" the principal shouted. "Next item please, Mrs. Laken."

"Next item. The assistant superintendent for personnel reported that they are still working on a salary chart for staff. They realize not all teachers have gotten their steps recently but they hope to have a working scale soon."

"I just found out," said a short teacher with bad hair, who stood up to speak. She taught sixth grade and I'd never spoken with her. "That I am making six hundred dollars more a year than these kids straight out of college. And I've been teaching twelve years."

Nods. Approval. Disgust. Several others had similar stories of working for many years and making a salary comparable to recent hires. What did the school board and personnel office intend to do about that? Mrs. Laken explained the salary chart was being hammered out for that purpose. Why were new employees being paid so well? Ms. Martin told the room that was between Human Resources and those employees. Taylor crossed her arms, arched an eyebrow, cocked her head and began staring down anyone who glanced her way. She began emitting a steady stream of quiet profanity.

"I deserve more than you," she said under her breath. "Old bag. I'm a better teacher than you, dumb 'ol bitch. You're old and washed up. Don't be mad at me because our school board sucks. Wrinkly old maid."

I felt this would be a bad time to indicate her current attitude hinted at why we wouldn't be good together. Maybe I'd email her. And then run.

Instead of picking a fight, I sat back and watched angry teachers take their frustrations with the school system's administration out on each other. They were mad enough to be violent.

38

Sunday night. Me, Kix, football, and nachos. It'd be perfect if Taylor was sitting on my lap. But. So far I'd resisted drinking that poison.

Mr. Cannon called. He'd have to do.

"Hey, Mack."

"Hey, Mr. Cannon. I'm ready for my weekly church update." Though not really. I needed a break from baptists.

"It was pretty good, pretty good," he said. "Pastor preached about the end times. Judgment day."

"Armageddon?"

"Armageddon happens before the Judgment Day," he said, sounding slightly annoyed and confused that I didn't already know that.

"I need to take some Bible classes."

"Well, hey, read Revelation. Real nice, real intense book. Judgment Day is when everyone, even the dead, is judged and eternity begins."

"I'm going to sweat a lot on that day," I said. Kix leaned back against my chest, his eyes slowly closing and bobbing open. Sleep was not far.

"I'll tell you what, though. Pastor avoided talking about the Bema Seat."

"What's the Bema Seat?" I asked, feeling justified about leaving my position at the church. What kind of youth minister doesn't know what the Bema Seat is? I hit Pause on my Tivo so I could listen.

"The Bema Seat is the second judgment, reserved for God's elect. God's chosen people will be rewarded for faithfulness, for serving Him."

"Excellent," I said. "I'm American so I'm very comfortable with being rewarded."

"Yeah, however, those who haven't followed God's will and haven't served Him will be judged."

"When does the Bema Seat happen?"

"After Judgment Day," he said, sounding confused again. "I'm surprised you don't know more about the Bema Seat."

"Why's that?"

"You were a preacher, for gosh sakes. And weren't you throwing people into jail to help God judge the wicked?"

"Matter fact, that is not why I did it," I said.

"Moses was sent into the desert, Mr. August, until he became ready to be God's warrior for His people. You have a purpose, just like Moses. Don't deny it or hide from it."

"My purpose might be teaching. I like teaching," I said.

"You are a fighter. You have God's fighting spirit. It's a real high calling. God's chosen people need everyone to do their part."

"God has a fighting spirit?"

"Read the Old Testament, Mr. August. God's enemies are destroyed."

Mr. Cannon struck me as someone who decided what God should be like and then viewed all the world through that lens. I didn't know if that was the right way or not, nor did I know if I had a lens. But if I did, it was different than his. "I'm still learning."

"Listen to God. He will speak to you," Cannon said.

"You ever talk with Mr. Suhr about this stuff?"

"The black man? Never."

"He's pretty spiritual," I said.

"Did the black man talk to you about pruning?"

"Negative."

"Those whom God loves He prunes," he said.

"Pruning! I remember that part. Hah, I'm not a total loss. Plus I recently helped Ms. Allen garden."

"Good. Our church is having a potluck this Wednesday. Let me know if you want to come."

I did not want to.

39

"**M**r. August," Mr. Suhr boomed out. He looked happy to see me. I'm likable. He sat behind a wooden workbench, screwdriver in hand, with what appeared to be the debris from a robotics explosion in front of him. An industrial-sized bendable lamp cast glares off the metal. His sleeves were rolled up and his tie was tucked into his shirt. He wore his brilliant white beard and smile. I stood in his doorway, wondering how I got there. "Please, come in."

I obeyed. His room felt very comforting, peaceful, manly. In this large, cavernous room full of tools and workbenches things were created. Robots and toys and projects were brainstormed and assembled. Creativity was harnessed and effort put forth and students watched their assignments take physical shape. I wished I could take his class and make things.

"As per my promise, I'm back."

"You're a man of your word," he said, and stood to shake my hand. "The Lord is with you, Mack August."

"And also with you," I said, and sat.

"Do you mean that?"

"I dunno. I respond out of habit."

"The Lord is with you," he repeated.

"Good to know."

"Are you still uncomfortable?" He smiled, picking up his screwdriver. "With conversations about what truly matters?"

"Wildly uncomfortable."

"America does not discuss the soul, because capitalism needs superficiality. Neither will your peers dialogue in depth with you, because it is not polite. You and I must be different, Mr. August. Because you were created for deeper things than televised singing competitions."

"I get it. Just not used to it yet."

"You will be someday. And then you will be the one forcing others to admit they have a soul."

"Tell me about the Bema Seat."

"The Bema Seat," he chuckled in surprise. I didn't blame him. He set his screwdriver back down. "Why do you ask that?"

"I heard about it recently. Curious."

"The Bema Seat is never directly mentioned in the Bible. Paul writes about a vague judgment in one of his letters, I forget which, I'm afraid. Not all Christians believe in it. In fact, I'd guess most don't."

"What do people like me believe?"

"Are you not a Christian?"

"I thought so. Before I moved here," I said. "Now I have no idea."

"Why not?"

"I'm not good at it. I don't like christians, often. They make me uncomfortable. I don't go to church. I don't listen to their music. I drink. I curse. Moving to the Bible Belt has intensified things."

"What do you think a christian is?"

"I have no idea, I guess. There seems to be quite a few definitions."

"You are correct," he said, nodding. "Good point. Let me ask you a question, young man. Is God a white American?"

I stopped myself before answering, "Of course." Ouch.

"I've always assumed God is similar to me," I said.

"You must avoid that. That is an incorrect and dangerous assumption. God made the people in California just like he made you. He also made the French, the Brazilians, and the New Zealanders."

"This is a hard concept to grasp, and I'm really smart. Way smarter than you."

"Is that right."

"So people who believe in the Bema Seat are nuts?"

"Maybe," he said, and then held up his finger at me. "More like... conservative. But don't judge them either. You eat your pizza one way, they eat theirs another. We are all made differently. We cannot afford to criticize each other. If you are doing so, you must stop. Do you understand? They are different than you, but not less valuable."

"Debatable. I heard recently that my purpose in life might be helping God throw his enemies into jail. That God has a fighting spirit and I was part of that."

He considered me for a long moment. He watched me, thinking, calmly, serenely.

"You been having strange conversations, Mr. August."

"I'll say. People in California only talk about television shows."

"The person who told you that has several misunderstandings. First, God loves everyone, even those who do not love Him back, so they should not be referred to as His enemies. Secondly, your purpose is to love God, and by extension his people. Lastly, God does not have a fighting spirit. He has a warrior spirit, which is different. The Lord is a warrior, not a fighter. A warrior keeps peace, and only fights for good when necessary."

"So, having a warrior's spirit isn't a bad thing."

"No, Mr. August. All tribes need warriors."

40

I ate breakfast, and on that particular morning it was a mistake. I needed the extra room for the students' writing projects. They picked their own topics for their How-To papers, and most of them choose dessert and all of them brought enough samples for everyone in the class. I sat immobile in my chair as third period planning started, and I had already eaten white chocolate covered pretzels, double chocolate chip cake, dirt cake, vanilla mudslide, cherry-flavored soda, fried chicken, and brownies. I still had three classes to go, and today was corndog nugget day in the cafeteria. I was doomed.

Near the end of planning, I emailed Mr. Charlie and invited myself to their next work night, and asked him why he hadn't mentioned these nights before. It occurred to me after I hit "Send" that I should have asked him this in person. Chocolate made me stupid, apparently.

Food kept pouring into the classroom and I kept eating it, grading the accompanying papers, and thinking about Mackenzie Allen. And Mr. Charlie, and work nights, and the mysterious note, and drugs, and South Hill, and the school board, and more drugs, and the shooter. Someone in Mecklenburg County was manufacturing crystal meth. Maybe several someones. Someone was also trafficking in cocaine. I bet these someones knew how to get their hands on hired muscle or a shooter if they needed one. But I didn't know how to get my hands on those someones, much less the shooters. I remained new to South Hill, an outsider. And the drug business didn't explain the note left in my room, nor why they would ace a middle school band teacher.

Charlie emailed me back right before eighth period ended, when I was almost in a food coma.

Mr. August, it's your lucky night. A few of us are meeting tonight to wipe down desks. Flu season is approaching and we can't be too careful. It should be a real good time. I'll meet you in front of your trailer at eight. We'll probably be here an hour tonight. Sincerely, Mr. Charlie

Bingo. I'd get to watch the usual crowd that Mr. Allen spent time with before he died. Nothing better for detecting guilt than hanging around and making people nervous.

I made a quick sweep of my room, throwing forks and plates into the auxiliary trash bag. The custodian gave me dirty looks because of my messy room, so I'd been making an effort. Hopefully I had gotten back onto his Christmas card list.

I motored a mile up to the high school. They had an open gym, which I visited now and then. A few of the beefier football players spotted me and followed me around the weights, challenging themselves to lift more than I could. A few of them succeeded. Two years ago I would have destroyed them, but I didn't mind the challenge nor the company. Good role models were hard to come by and I made sure my life was very transparent, easy to inspect and imitate. I answered their questions, joked with them, encouraged them, got very honest concerning my mistakes. A couple even left the gym to run a few laps around the track with me. I finished and decided I'd probably ran off two periods' worth of dessert and the rest would go straight to my ass.

After toweling dry in the locker room, I used the shower-in-a-bottle spray which guaranteed I'd get more girls, and went to Leta and James's house for dinner. Kix's babysitters were the closest thing to family I had for two hundred miles. I drank iced tea and tried to burn calories by concentrating. Kix could feed himself now, which made eating much more enjoyable and cleanup much more of a hassle. Most of his macaroni ended up on his cheeks and eyebrows, and between handfuls he would often offer me a bite. My heart swelled with pride at my generous and disgusting child.

Leta rejoiced at the opportunity to keep Kix a few more hours while I was at the school with Mr. Charlie and his work night crew. Her son lived four hundred miles away and only visited on holidays. So I left Kix there and drove back to the middle school, ready to clean desks.

As I drove I thought about how the investigation kept getting in the way of quality time with Kix. We still had most nights together and the weekends, but I felt bad when I only saw him for a few minutes like I would today. Yet another reason to bag the killer.

I got there a little before eight. One car in the lot. It was dark enough for the street and courtyard lights to have turned on, bathing the brick buildings and sidewalks in orange. I pulled into a space close to the entrance and killed the engine. Something felt wrong. Then I saw the body.

Same place as last time, lying in roughly the same position. The hairs on my neck stood up. I reached over and removed a gun from the glove compartment. I owned two guns, and felt very satisfied with my decision to keep one in the car. Just a small Smith and Wesson .38 Special, but it'd do the trick.

I fought off the notion that I was a hypocrite. After all, I told the resource officer to put away his gun that morning. But that had been seven in the morning and this was eight at night. Nighttime was way scarier, after all, a scientific fact. And this was the second body. And I was alone. Hypocrite or not, I got out of the car armed.

I approached cautiously, peering as best I could into the shadows of the courtyard, but there were too many places someone could hide and watch. I knew the corpse was a man and I knew he was dead, but I got close enough to confirm anyway. And close enough to realize I knew him.

I'd grown tired of dialing 911, so instead I punched in the sheriff's cell.

"Yeah."

"Hey, it's Mack August."

"Yeah?" he asked.

"Got another body. Same place as last time."

"You gotta be kiddin' me."

"I wish."

"Christ, why do people keep dying around you?"

I hung up and tried to pretend that wasn't true.

41

I looked at my watch every fifteen seconds for the next six minutes. After two of them my thighs began to burn but I didn't shift positions. My pistol lay between my feet and if someone wanted to shoot me they could.

Roy had been shot in the forehead at close range with a small caliber pistol. It appeared that he'd fallen dead where he currently lay and hadn't been moved, unlike Mackenzie Allen. Other than that, a bunch of little signs pointed to the same shooter. The back of his head was bloody and his hands were still in his pockets. He'd taken one in the forehead and fallen backwards, dead before he hit the asphalt.

If this trend continued then we'd run out of faculty soon. I'd be the last teacher standing.

He stared into space, a look of vacant surprise in his eyes. I stared at him as memories of other corpses superimposed themselves onto his body. I could hear the sounds of Los Angeles, smell gunpowder, feel blood on my hands, hear myself and others crying, hear the sirens coming closer.

His body took on a flickering bluish hue and two squad cars rolled into the parking lot. One pulled up onto the sidewalk, as close to the courtyard as it could get, and illuminated everything with its high beams. I stood and kept my hands by my sides so they could see them. Car doors slammed.

I recognized Detective Andrews by his voice. "Shit. Same as last time. Same as freakin' last time."

"That's my piece," I said. "On the ground. I took it out of the car when I saw the body."

"Yeah, well put it back. You look guilty enough as it is."

I retrieved the revolver and put it in my jacket pocket.

"What are you doing here so late, anyway?" he asked.

"I was just wondering the same thing."

DUE TO THE CIRCUMSTANCES, there was a noticeable attitude shift toward me. I no longer held the position of helpful former detective. Now I was a potential suspect. I knew both victims, I'd found both bodies, and, considering the small-town nature of South Hill, everyone already knew Roy didn't like me. I went from insider to outsider, and the looks I got from the deputies confirmed it. And what was I doing at the school so late?

Sheriff Mitchell arrived and asked that exact question. I told him about the work nights. So where was everybody? I resisted the urge to say, "Dead."

"So you know about these late-night cleaning parties?" Sheriff Mitchell asked.

Principal Martin nodded. She'd arrived fifteen minutes after the sheriff. She wore Crocks, jeans and a college sweatshirt. The three of us stood in her office. The hallways were dark. Her desk light was burning. "One of the administrators has to be here. I didn't know about it tonight."

The sheriff's arms were crossed. He turned his gaze to me.

"I didn't know about it either until Mr. Charlie told me this afternoon," I said.

"Is Roy Davis usually at these meetings?"

"Sometimes," she said. "Yes."

"Sheriff," a deputy said, sticking his head in the room. He was running messages into the room every few minutes. "Officers Crossman and Carley are here."

"Have them start knocking on doors," he said, arms still crossed. "See if anyone heard or saw anything."

"Yessir." He disappeared.

"The last meeting, or party, or cleaning party, or whatever. When was it?" he asked.

"No idea. I found out about these parties yesterday," I said.

"Last month sometime," Principal Martin said, and she bent over her desk to look through her calendar.

"Who told you about the parties?"

"Mackenzie Allen's mother," I sighed. I usually asked the questions. I felt frustrated being on the other side. "She came to visit me, see how the investigation was going."

"What'd you tell her?"

"I said I'd kill Roy if it'd make her feel better."

"Think you're funny?"

"Think you're being productive?"

"Gentlemen." Ms. Martin rubbed her forehead. "Not now. The last meeting was September twenty-fifth."

"Who was there?"

"I'm not sure," she said. "I wasn't. I'd guess Mr. Charlie, Mr. Allen, Ms. Smith, Ms. Lewis, Mr. Davis, Mr. Gosney probably, a few of the custodians most likely. And Vice Principal Mr. Baskins."

I made a mental list of the names. Future leads, perhaps.

"Both victims are in that list," I said.

"Think it's a clue, hotshot?" he said.

Detective Andrews entered the office. "Sir? Mr. Charlie is here."

"And?"

"He says there was no cleaning scheduled tonight. And he never emailed August."

All three stared at me.

"Ah hah!"

"Ah hah?"

"A clue," I said. I could see it in their eyes. Who was lying? Me or Charlie? "This is easy to verify. Mind if I use your computer?"

Martin logged herself off and I sat down. I logged on. I hadn't deleted Charlie's email, and even if I had the letter would still be in the Trash. I pulled up the program.

The emails were listed in chronological order. At the top was the most recent email. The letter at the top of my email program was a note from the nurse, sent an hour before Charlie had sent his. No letter from Charlie. I checked the Trash folder. Nothing. In other words, my alibi was gone.

"Where is it?" the sheriff asked.

"Not there," I said. "Now that, Sheriff, is suspicious."

42

I was upgraded to a Person of Interest in the investigation. Charlie came in to confirm he hadn't sent the email, and he gave all indications of telling the truth. I expected him to fidget, ramble too much, look to his left, shuffle his feet, not know what to do with his hands. He was either a pro, or honestly hadn't sent that email. The principal deliberately kept her distance from me.

The sheriff went to deal with the crime scene and I decided to wait in a classroom near the exit closest to the courtyard. Leaving would make the sheriff nervous, as he wasn't sure if he trusted me or not. Besides, I wanted to figure out where that email went and I had access to a computer. Whatever happened to that email would point to the actual perpetrator. The classroom belonged to a sixth-grade teacher who pasted motivational posters and catchy science phrases on her walls.

This time the story might go national. Two teachers, same school, same location, probably the same gun. The leap from one murder to two was a big one, and the public would be fascinated with public servants being murdered at their job. The press would invade South Hill in a much bigger way than last time, and the public and parent outcry was going to triple.

I pushed away from the computer in frustration. I didn't know enough about computers to investigate the disappearing email very far. It was gone. That's what I knew. I lowered my head into my hands and tried to think.

Mackenzie Allen. Band teacher. Roy Davis. Agriculture teacher. Both liked Taylor. Both had potential beef with the school board, and vice-versa. Both participated in the work nights or cleaning parties. Killed in very similar styles. What was Roy doing at the school tonight?

Definite similarities. How did I fit in? Why did I get a bogus email? Or did I? Why did Charlie never mention those cleaning parties before? Where was Russ Cummings tonight? What about that mysterious note?

Until I cleared my name, I couldn't help answer those questions. Suspects are strongly discouraged from interfering with homicide investigations. But I wasn't sure how to clear my name without answering some of those questions. I bounced my head on the heels of my hands and said, "Think, think, think."

"Think about what, Mr. August?"

I looked up as Mr. Suhr walked into the room.

"You live nearby?" I asked. Seeing a friendly face was not unpleasant.

"I volunteer on the Rescue Squad. We are going to transport the body later tonight. I heard you were in here and decided I would come tell you that the Lord is still with you."

"Doesn't feel like it," I said.

"Do you always determine truth by what you feel?"

I put my head back into my hands.

"I know it was not you," he said. "I know you're not the killer."

"That makes one of us."

"Anyone who knows you will not believe it was you."

"They have nothing beyond circumstantial evidence. I'm not worried about that. Frustrated, yes. Worried, no."

"Then what are you worried about? You look badly shaken," he said.

"Finding the body," I said. "Shook me up."

"I assumed a police officer who investigated homicides for a living would be used to bodies. Were you and Roy close?"

"No. Not that, really," I said.

"Then what?"

"Memories. The last few bodies have brought memories and nightmares. I was involved in the North murders, a grisly ordeal."

We stared through the classroom windows into the courtyard for a minute. I couldn't see the body but I could see a deputy taking pictures, his flash and the blue siren lights lighting up my trailer in the background.

"Every corpse I see turns into my best friend's body. His name was Richard. He was my partner."

Mr. Suhr nodded but didn't say anything.

"He was shot in front of me. I held him as he died. My life didn't make sense after that, and I lost my ability to effectively do my job."

"I can understand," he said in his big, tall, kind drawl.

"To make matters worse," I said. "His wife was pregnant. But here is the really weird thing. Richard was sterile, so they asked if I would donate sperm and be the biological father. I was very tight with them, so of course I said yes. Then he died, and his wife Melynda went to pieces. She lost her will to live, couldn't get out of bed. Clinically depressed and suicidal, but she was pregnant and didn't want to take powerful drugs. She couldn't even muster up the energy to push during delivery, and she died right after an emergency C-section. While I held her hand. No one else was there, so they handed the baby to me. I was the biological father, so no one thought much about it. All that in the same month. So now when I see a body I remember holding Richard as he bled to death with an ambulance not far away, and I remember Melynda dying on the operating table."

He whistled and shook his head, then said, "Those are significant memories."

"Yup."

"What help have you received?"

"Counseling helped. Drinking, sex and overeating did not."

"That does not surprise me."

"All this...shit inside of me. I'm still polluted from those years of self-destruction. Memories, you know? Awful memories. Dunno how to get rid of them."

"It is a process," he said. "I work Rescue Squad. I know. You were damaged physically and spiritually."

"Not sure about the spiritual part."

"You think murder is not a spiritual problem?"

"I guess it is," I said, rubbing my eyes with the heels of my hands. "I investigated homicides for several years and I never thought about it spiritually."

"How many murders went unsolved in or around your city while you were there?" he asked.

"Many."

"Maybe that is because the investigators only think in terms of what they can see. Maybe you are still doing it."

"Mr. Suhr, I'm too tired for this."

"I know, but I believe you are more involved in these murders than you think."

I didn't answer. Did he know I'd received a note from the killer?

He continued, "Perhaps because I know nothing about the evidence and therefore necessarily am not influenced by it, but I've been praying for you. And while I pray, I grow more and more aware that you are involved and in danger."

"You're a creepy guy, Mr. Suhr. I don't know if I can believe that spiritual forces are the key to solving murders."

"You used to not believe in God. Does that mean He did not exist then?"

"No, I think He existed whether or not I believed."

"Then trust me on this, Mr. August. There is more going on here than what can be seen."

I rubbed my forehead and watched the lights outside. "I don't get it. I'm trying."

"The police are good at what they do. In fact, government and justice are both ideas from God. But they are not investigating this from a spiritual standpoint. Do not put your trust in the police. Put your trust in a higher power."

"And I'm involved?"

"I think so."

"How?" I asked.

"I do not know."

"Is the school board involved?"

"I do not know," he said. "I am not a prophet or a psychic. I only know that I feel very burdened to warn you and pray for you."

"So," I said, leaning back in my chair and trying not to feel foolish, "if this has something to do with influences we can't see, and involves me..." I let the gears in my mind turn. Was I looking in the wrong place? Ignoring something? "...then I bet I know where another clue is."

"How do I help?"

"Fetch the sheriff."

Mr. Suhr left, and five minutes later he returned.

"You need to see me?" the sheriff said.

"Yep. Time to come clean."

"Yeah?"

"I got a note from the killer. I think so, at least."

He arched an eyebrow, crossed his arms, and didn't say anything.

"The first school day after Allen's death, I found a note on my keyboard. It's currently in the top right desk drawer in my trailer. It warned me to be careful with whom I'm friends."

"Whom?"

"Yup. Whom."

"Why didn't you share this before?" he asked.

"I didn't want word to get out. If I shared it with you it might become common knowledge and scare the guy off."

"Thanks for the vote of confidence."

"I shipped it to LA for finger prints, my old outfit," I said. "You can call them to confirm. The note is a standard index card with pasted magazine letters. No prints anywhere."

"We could have used this information two weeks ago."

"Maybe," I said.

"I could bust you for impeding a police investigation."

"Maybe."

"So why tell me now?"

"I gotta funny feeling," I said. "There might be another note on my keyboard."

43

The following day was Saturday. No school, so Kix and I practiced crawling. I owned several books on being a father and raising a boy, but none of them gave advice for crawling exercises. I did, however, feel confident in my ability to give the sex talk when he turned ten. In the meantime, I laid him stomach down on the carpet and placed bits of cookie just out of his reach. He possessed the ability to squirm his way forward and get the cookie, but nothing approached crawling. He was developing a mean scowl because I kept moving the cookie backwards.

I hadn't stayed long at the school the previous night. The sheriff had returned to the classroom rattled, holding a second note. Same style of note card, same cutout magazine letters. Different message.

YOUR FRIEND SELECTION IS POOR.

My planning and suspicions were down the tubes. The school board theory now looked weak. Roy was dead, so it probably wasn't him. The work night angle was all weird. Maybe one of them, maybe not, and I couldn't imagine it could be Mr. Charlie. Everything now hinged on that email and the two notes.

Two dead bodies, both lying in front of my trailer. Two murders, two notes, both seemingly addressed to me. The implications of that were something I didn't enjoy thinking about.

Before leaving the school, I had called an old friend in LA and asked if we could send her some things to look at. She was a pro, and I'd feel better with her opinion on the evidence.

Kix and I walked around the house for a while. He held my two pointer fingers and took long, wobbly steps through the kitchen and living room while bragging about himself loudly.

The sheriff's department was running fingerprints, processing the body, casing the school campus, going over film from the school's cameras, comparing notes from the Allen homicide, and trying to catch a killer. I was duck walking with my son.

I still remained under a fair amount of suspicion due to my shady email alibi. Until that mystery was solved the sheriff couldn't be sure I hadn't left those notes myself, however unlikely. To make matters worse, the local newspaper had a nasty habit of discovering and printing all the investigation details. It wouldn't be long before my picture adorned the front page, subtitled "Suspect." That would not help the teacher-parent relationship. I intentionally did not watch the news, confident Richmond and Raleigh would run it, as probably would a few twenty-four-hour cable news shows.

I made us PBJ sandwiches for lunch. After we finished eating, I was going to drop Kix off at Leta's and head to the sheriff's office. Considering the killer appeared to be interested in me, and I had more experience with homicides than all law enforcers in South Hill combined, it seemed reasonable that I should help out. They'd accept my help more willingly if I had a good explanation for being at school so late last night. For the tenth time, I wished I'd printed out that email.

Kix smeared his food onto his face and managed to get some in his mouth while I opened up my laptop. I'd begun an email earlier to my father, filling him in so he wouldn't worry. The screen with the half-finished letter was there waiting for me after the computer returned from hibernation. I stared at the screen for a while, trying to figure out what exactly was nagging me. I felt I was missing something obvious. Unable to locate the source, I finished the letter and hit "Send." The email disappeared, leaving the In-box on screen.

"Ah hah."

Kix smiled at me.

"Daddy's got an idea."

About time, he said.

I CALLED the sheriff's office and was quickly transferred.

"Sheriff Mitchell.

"Yes, I have a legal question. Would I get into less trouble for shooting a cat rather than a dog? And can I borrow your gun? Don't ask what for."

"Who the hell is this?"

"Your favorite middle school teacher. When I check my emails at school, those emails pop up in separate, individual windows on my monitor. They stay there on screen until I close out the window or reply to them. Make sense?"

"Yeah, so."

"The email from Mr. Charlie was the last thing I saw on my screen yesterday. I don't think I cancelled it out. Even though the school's email server has no record of that email, I think there will be a copy of it on my screen."

"I'll ask the principal to meet one of my deputies there and open the door. He'll take a look."

"You'll need my password to unlock the screensaver," I said.

"Okay," he said. "Let me write it down."

"This is a little embarrassing."

"Get over it, August," he responded. "You're a person of interest in a murder investigation."

"All right, fine. It's 'Sheriff Mitchell.'"

"Christ, I'm thinking about throwing you into jail just to shut you up."

I gave him the correct password and got Kix dressed. He liked to lie on his back, kick his legs and laugh while I tried to thread his legs into his pants. I bet Sheriff Mitchell would threaten to throw him in jail if he saw.

Leta forced a BLT sandwich on me when we got to her house. Even though the grass had stopped growing two weeks ago, James was on his riding lawn mower and he waved as I drove off. He'd recently decided he didn't want me to catch the killer, he wanted me to shoot him. Better yet, catch the killer, bring him to James and let James shoot him. I'd get free babysitting for a month. I listened to a sermon on the radio, discussing the Song of Solomon. According to the preacher, I'd been all messed up when it came to women, and I had a feeling he was right. I also became pretty sure that Taylor was not the girl for me, no matter what she looked like in heels. I just had to avoid touching her the rest of the school year. The thought of being successful in my next relationship filled me with hope. If there was a next relationship.

44

I parked in front of the sheriff's office and walked in. The Mecklenburg County law enforcers were on edge. The front secretary was on the phone and probably had been all day, fielding calls from press. An open newspaper lay on a tabletop. The homicide had just enough time to make the front page, but the report was scarce with developing details. I was mentioned. Third time in about three weeks.

Detective Andrews waved me in. His clipboard was on his desk, pencil lying on top. His hair looked great.

"Identical to Mackenzie Allen," he said. "Roy Davis drove himself to school, no sign of struggle, same slug, assuming same gun which we'll verify soon, tissue cleaned up the blood. Davis wasn't moved though. That's the only difference."

"Cell phone clean?"

"Nothing suspicious. None of his recent calls matched Allen's."

"I'd check house phones or look for another cell. Both these guys had to be communicating with someone somehow. They were both at the school late, and someone apparently knew they were coming. If not a phone or email, then face to face?"

"We're bringing in school staff. Starting later today. We'll ask them if they ever saw those two hanging out with the same people, but that'll be tough to narrow down."

"His wife Marie have anything interesting to say?" I asked.

"Yes."

That's all he said. He was enjoying this. I played along.

"And?"

"Marie said Roy went out drinking after dinner, like usual. Before he left, he told her he'd be back late. Said he had to help some friends at the school."

"Ah hah. A work night. Did Roy's wife say which friends he was supposed to meet?"

"Yep."

"Fine. I'll guess. Elvis?"

"Mr. Charlie and Taylor Williams," he said.

"That so?"

"That is so." He nodded.

"I bet Marie's ready to kill Taylor."

"She had a loaded gun on the table. So why did Roy Davis think Charlie and Williams would be at the school so late?"

"Same reason I did, maybe," I said.

"Charlie is starting to look suspicious."

"It's not Charlie," I said.

"How do you know?"

"I can tell."

"Oh. You can tell." He smiled. "Pardon me. I didn't realize you could tell."

"He wasn't lying about that email. And we've talked before. I can smell guilt."

"Fascinating," the sheriff said, walking into the room. Andrews got up and sat in another chair. Sheriff Mitchell sat down in the vacant chair, pulled out a drawer and rested his boots on it. "What a fascinating superhero power. You can be Captain Super Nose. Okay with you if I question him anyway, Captain?"

"You look tense. You need a back rub?"

The Sheriff stared passively at me until Deputy Burnette walked in. I recognized her from the myriad of crime scenes I'd been at recently. She was dressed in deputy-brown and her hair was braided.

"Got it," she said. "The first thing on this sucker's computer screen was an email from Mr. Charlie. Maybe he wasn't lying after all." She handed over a printed copy of the email.

"You look nice, are you braiding your hair differently?" I asked.

"Be nice if you was guilty," she said, not looking at me. "Could rough you up. And shut you up."

"Real nice," Mitchell agreed, reading the copy of the email I'd been bragging about. "So," he said after a second read. "It's not you."

"It's not me."

"Then who is it?"

"Someone with access to the school's email server," I said.

"And why do they keep dropping bodies in front of your trailer and leaving you notes?" he asked.

"Cause I'm lovable?"

"Let me throw him in jail," she said. "Just for a little while."

"Deputy Burnette," Mitchell said. "Run background checks on all staff at South Hill Middle. Call the principal and find out who had master keys or access to the school's email server. Start with them."

"I'd include all public school technology employees in your background searches, not just those at our particular school," I said.

"Fine. That too."

"Red flag anyone who lives near the school," I said. "This person is getting to the school regularly, so they'll probably live close."

The sheriff nodded.

"Yes sir," she said, and she walked out.

"Can I borrow a phone? I want to call a friend."

"Your forensic psychologist?" Andrews asked.

"Yup," I said.

"Call here. I'm listening. Andrews," he said. "Take notes."

We surrounded the sheriff's phone. I punched in a number and put it on speaker.

"Hello," a woman's voice said.

"Hi Anne," I said.

"Mackenzie, my boy!" she said, so loudly the speakerphone vibrated a little on the desk. Anne Parker was a forensic psychologist contracted out by the LAPD. We'd collaborated on the high-profile North murders. She had also been fairly unprofessional in her pursuit of me, which I'd found both distasteful and charming. Couldn't blame her though, poor girl. "Two phone calls in two days. I'm blushing."

"Long distance, no less."

"And you didn't even call collect. I knew we were meant to be together."

"Anne, did you get..."

"You have a computer nearby? We could video conference and watch each other while we talk dirty."

"This is your criminal profiler?" Sheriff Mitchell asked me.

"Should I be taking notes on this part?" Andrews said.

"Am I on speaker?" she asked.

"Maybe," I said.

"You bad boy," she said. "What kind of girl do you think I am?"

"Did you get a chance to look at all those pictures and notes we sent your way?"

"Of course, Mackenzie. Anything for you," she said, and we could hear her start clicking on her computer. "Let me pull my notes up." The three of us looked at each other, waited, and had an unspoken "Who's Tougher" competition. At least I did. I won. "These old computers. Are you dating anyone?"

"No ma'am."

Andrews coughed, but it sounded like his cough was less a result of an irritant within his lungs and more as a contradiction to my statement.

"Whaaaat?" Anne said. "Is this true? You're dating? I'm hanging up. No wait, here they are. Ready?"

"Shoot."

"Bear in mind, love, that I've only had these a few hours and I know next to nothing about the case. I may tell you nothing new. But here goes.

"As you know, crime scenes tell us an awful lot about the person who committed them. The body being dragged, the tissue cleaning up blood, the lack of shells, the lack of noise, the emails, all this points to a very neat, tidy, thorough individual. Murder weapon is strange, and considering how systematic this guy is he might have bored his own revolver barrel to fit the silencer. I'm saying 'he' because odds are it's a white male. But that's just the odds.

"The note's your biggest clue. It's fascinating for several reasons. First, it's written in very proper English. Highly unusual, so not only is he thorough and careful but also educated. Second, it's not signed. Notes from the killer are usually signed. Third, notes are almost always intended for the media or the police.

"Considering the bodies were left outside your classroom, considering the notes were left for you and not to get attention from the public, considering the notes were both criticizing and warning you about who your friends are, this killer might be taking a ride on the Obsessive Love Wheel."

"Uh oh," I said.

"The what?" Sheriff Mitchell asked. Andrews wrote as fast as he could.

"Obsessions generally follow a predictable pattern. Attraction, anxiety, obsession, destruction. Those four make up the Obsessive Love Wheel. The killings and notes sound to me like the obsession and destruction phases."

"So a lunatic is in love with August? That your guess? A gay lunatic?"

"Not necessarily romantic love," I said, and I rubbed my eyes.

"Mack's right," she said. "Most likely, yes, a romantic obsession. But not necessarily. So our male profile is either gay or has a non-romantic obsession with him."

"Or," I said. "It's a woman."

"Or it's a woman," she agreed. "It appears to me that the murderer has tunnel vision with Mack and is using extreme control tactics, along with the anger, rage and revenge associated with the destructive phase."

"It's probably because I'm so funny."

"Mack, any love interests or friends acting obsessive?" she asked.

"Other than you?"

"Other than me," Anne said, a smile obvious in her voice over the phone.

"Nope."

"You said you were dating," she prompted.

"No, Captain America coughed that I am dating. She was no big deal."

"She still pursuing you? What about new friends? If this is an obsession, it's probably a recent relationship. Considering the anonymous nature of the notes, there's a good chance this person does not want their obsession discovered, which would fit their careful personality. He or she wants to be close to you but doesn't want you to know he's obsessed. I'm surprised this hadn't occurred to you, Mack."

"I think I didn't want it to occur to me."

"So why kill Allen and Davis?" Mitchell asked.

"That's why I'm not sure it's a romantic obsession," I said. "I wasn't romantically involved with those two. Just friends. No romantic competition," I said.

"Maybe," Anne said. "I have to run, boys. Because of my love for you, Mack, I'll keep glancing at this and re-sifting my thoughts."

"Thanks," I said, and she hung up.

We sat in silence, processing. If she was right, and the evidence was quickly ruling out most other options, then the list of suspects just got very small.

"So," Detective Andrews said. "Is it Taylor? She the killer?" He looked worried. I didn't blame him, considering two other guys whom she flirted with had recently been aced.

"Yeah," Mitchell said. "What's your super nose tell you?"

"One thing is for certain. Whoever this person is," I said, "they have superior taste."

SOUTH HILL MIDDLE SCHOOL staff began showing up for questioning. First through the door walked Taylor. I disappeared in a back room. I didn't want her or Mr. Charlie to see me and develop suspicions.

I remained very curious about the emails. If emails sent to me had been deleted, what else had been erased? If Charlie hadn't sent that email, which was still up for debate, then how many other fake emails had been sent? It certainly appeared that one had been sent to Roy Davis.

Using an old machine in the back, I searched staff directories online for South Hill Middle's technology resource staff person. Her name was Emily Newman. I dialed her home, got a machine, and left a message asking her to call me.

Rain began to sound outside.

I was still in the back room, looking through pictures, when Russ Cummings walked in. Russ Cummings the school board member.

"Mr. August," he said, and held out his hand. He wore a three-button charcoal suit and tasseled shoes. I wondered if his ring cost more than my car. He did not smile. "Good to see you."

I shook his hand and nodded.

He sat down beside me, rested one hand on his knee and rubbed his forehead with a handkerchief with the other.

"I just came by to see how the investigation was coming. Another one of our teachers..." he said and shook his head. No faking, he was genuinely upset. "Listen, about what we talked about? On the golf course? Forget it," he said, and fixed me with his eyes. "Just find the fucker. Forget what I said."

I nodded and said, "Already forgotten."

He nodded too, patted me on the knee, looked like he wanted to say something else but instead he walked out.

So now my school board theory lay in ruins. Rain beat against the back window.

Detective Andrews came to get me an hour later.

"Questioning is done for the day," he said, scratching a thirty-six-hour beard. "Hopefully the medical examiner will be completely finished in the morning. And maybe we'll get back the ballistics report.

"Nothing special turned up during questioning, but you can grill the sheriff for details. Not many have great alibis, a few are going to check email timestamps or internet conversations and get back to me, including Mr. Charlie and Taylor Williams. A digital alibi is better than nothing. It's been a long couple days, I'm going home for dinner," he said, and he left.

I followed him out, my stomach growling, and noticed Deputy Burnette had personnel files open on her desk.

"You have cell phone numbers?" I asked.

"Mm-hm."

"See if Emily Newman has one. She's Technology Resources."

She did. I got it and left. A rainy night had fallen and I went to get Kix.

45

Kix waved at me sleepily in the rearview mirror as we pulled away from James's and Leta's house around 7:30 pm. The time would be changing soon but it was already dark, and my windshield wipers steadily churned.

I punched in Emily Newman's cell. She answered it on the second ring.

"Hello?"

"Ms. Newman, this is Mack August. English teacher, eighth grade."

"Oh, hi! You don't remember me, but I helped you set up your electronic grade book right after you were hired."

"I do remember you." I did. Happy lady, smiled a lot. "I'm helping the sheriff's office with the homicide investigation. Have you heard from the sheriff or Detective Andrews yet?"

"Yes, I did, just a little while ago."

"Super. Got a question for you. I believe I received a bogus email earlier this week, but it was deleted. It wasn't in my trash bin either, but it was sent to me from Mr. Charlie's email account. It would be helpful to know whether Charlie still has a copy of that email in his

Sent folder. Basically, I need to know, was that email sent from Charlie's account or did it originate elsewhere?"

"I can do better than that, Mr. August. I can locate that email and verify its sender, whether or not it's still in his Sent folder," she said.

"How do you do that?"

"Because emails are a gray area. Do they belong to the county or not? We play it safe and keep all emails at central office, both sent and received. We can't read them unless they are flagged for inappropriate content or if we are required to. For example, in a homicide investigation. But we have copies of them all."

"Emily," I said. "I could've used that information yesterday. Saved me a sleepless night, and cleared my name quicker."

"Sorry!"

"You can't access the central office's email log from home, can you?"

"No. You have to be at school."

"Okay. We'll answer those questions tomorrow, then."

"I'm at the school now," she said. "Can I help with anything?"

A small alarm went off in my head.

"Why are you at the school?" I asked.

"The sheriff called me, like I told you. He's going to meet me here and look at the emails you just mentioned."

I was cruising along Route One at fifty miles per hour. I pinched the phone between my shoulder and ear, dropped a gear, mashed the gas, cut the wheel, and spun a perfect U-turn.

"Emily, I'm four miles away and I'm coming to pick you up," I said, pushing into the next gear. I was redlining between each shift. "Is there a back door?"

"I think so. Why? Hang on a second." I could hear her moving around. "I'm back here!" she yelled away from the phone.

"Emily!" I shouted, and Kix startled in the backseat

"What's wrong? I think the sheriff just get here."

"Listen to me, Emily. That's not the sheriff. He went home." She gasped and the noises stopped. "Do what I say, else you'll be dead when I get there. If there's a back door, use it and run. If not, hide. Put your phone on vibrate. I'm hanging up and calling the police," I said and I hit End.

I punched in 911, which I should probably put on speed dial. I was doing eighty around curves, and fishtailed around a stop sign onto Highway 58. The golf clubs in my trunk were sliding everywhere. Two miles away.

The killer had lured the technology resource teacher to the email server at school. I bet he was guessing he could manipulate emails and erase evidence from that server. I filled the 911 operator in on what was happening. She contacted the sheriff's office and put out a radio call. I was the closest to the school by several miles.

I power-slid as best a Honda Accord could manage around the final stop sign, turning right onto the street leading to the middle school. My Highway Patrol training put me at the school a least a minute faster. South Hill Middle is long, most of the school being visible from the large front parking lot. The front entrance glowed with spotlights; the north and south exits had streetlights; and the back of the school had a few well-lit spots. Other than that, most of the building and campus remained dark.

There was one car in the parking lot. My tires crunched and scudded as I braked hard to stop, facing the building from the parking lot entrance. I rolled down the window, but all I could hear was the engine growling down to a steady idle and the rain. After the rush to get here, the night sounded eerily quiet. The air felt cold compared to the warm car.

Emily was crouching behind a bush near the front entrance. She didn't realize the school's spotlight was hitting her so directly. I'd have to drive forward fifty yards through the parking lot approaching the school, until the car was directly in front of the right-hand entrance, and turn left and drive another hundred yards to reach her hiding spot. I'd be following the route taken by the school buses, basically, as they loaded and unloaded students. The car would be within spitting distance of the school, an easy target. The sound of the rain hammering the roof of the car increased. My tires smelled hot.

Slowly, I eased the car forward. When I got close enough, I'd gun it, but until then I wanted silence. My eyes were no longer on Emily, but were scanning the shadows.

I redialed her number. She answered and breathed heavy into the phone without saying anything.

"I'm in the car," I said. "When I get close enough, run for the passenger door. If you hear a gunshot, jump through the passenger window and hold on."

Movement, out of the corner of my eye. In the shadows, close to the wall, dead ahead of me. The killer? I couldn't get to Emily without driving right by that spot. Nor could Emily get to her own car.

I mashed the gas, and loose parking lot gravel sprayed. New plan: run over the shooter. I'd be an easy target for the next forty-five yards, but he'd have to be a world-class shot to get me. Calculated risk.

Except...

The brakes squealed, the engine quieted, and the car stopped.

Kix. I'd forgotten he slipped in and out of sleep in the backseat. No calculated risk was worth him.

I ground my teeth in frustration. I was sitting still too long, making myself vulnerable, but I didn't know what to do.

First priority, Kix stays alive. Second, so does Emily. Third, catch the shooter.

"Emily," I said into the phone. "I see him. He's near the southern entrance, between you and your car. My kid is in the backseat, so I'm bailing out and chasing him down on foot. I need you to drive my car and get Kix to safety. It's much closer than your car. Get out of range and wait for the police."

I hit the gas again, cut the wheel, and re-aimed. The high beams flooded the area where I'd seen someone. More movement. A flash of a body ducking behind a shrub, moving backwards into the quad. Maybe I imagined it, but I might have seen the glint of gunmetal.

I shoved open the door and yelled, "Go!"

A gun fired.

I needed no extra motivation. A bullet could hit my car and my son. My feet pounded faster than I thought possible.

A second gunshot and a small muzzle flash. Instinctively, I winced and leaped mid-step. I was thirty yards from the school and too far for an amateur to hit a moving target with a revolver in the rain. He wasn't using a silencer, I noted as I flew over the sidewalk. I hadn't been shot at in a long time. I still hated it.

Closer, closer. I was moving too fast to check on Emily. If she wasn't running to the car then she and I were going to have words later.

I reached the quad sidewalk, planted a foot, changed directions, and slashed diagonally to the right. Just in time. Another muzzle flash, another ear splitting crash. If he was using a six-shot revolver, he only had three bullets left.

I'd forgotten my gun in the excitement. Brilliant.

I slid and came to a complete stop, hitting the side of the school. The shooter retreated backwards from the entrance, deeper into the school campus and closer to my trailer. He could hide behind the brick columns or retreat further and shoot from around the corner of a trailer. Meanwhile the headlights were going to silhouette me if I ran after him. I wiped water out of my eyes.

A car door slammed. Gears ground and my car began to haltingly reverse. Way to go, Emily. The Honda lights swung away from the courtyard entrance, pitching me into darkness.

Sirens wailed in the distance.

I counted to three and went on two. I ran into the courtyard and at the last minute I ducked behind the final brick column. Another gunshot, the retort growing louder and echoing against the bricks. The bullet sounded like a whip as it tore violently through the decorative bushes. I didn't see the muzzle flash but I guessed the shooter was behind a trailer. My trailer. Only two bullets left. If he was using a revolver.

He could easily flank me and shoot around the column so I left my hiding spot in a hurry. As I did, the fifth bullet snapped into the bricks beside my head, shattering and sending splinters flying. They clawed at my face, but I kept running, spurred on by the sixth gunshot, which destroyed a rear-facing window in the school.

The silhouette of the shooter was black against the gray night. I made it safely to the trailer. I was on one side, he was on the other. The sirens got louder.

Did he have a revolver or not? If he did, he was out of bullets and needed to reload, which would take precious seconds. I planned to use those seconds to my advantage. I mustered my courage, edged my way around the corner of the trailer and ran down the length.

I lowered my shoulder, turned the final corner, and charged. No one there. Gone. I stepped onto six golden shell casings, which rolled on the sidewalk. Dropped seconds ago.

The shooter could have gone several directions. If I spent much time guessing he could shoot me from the shadows, so I picked a direction and ran.

I guessed wrong. The baseball field was big and faintly illuminated with hazy moonlight through the rain. I splashed to a stop at the fence. Not this way.

Turning, I saw the shooter. A hundred yards distant. I'd run directly away from him. He was moving full speed, leaving the school grounds, but I could see an outline. The figure was thin and not very tall. I soon lost sight of him in the shadows.

For a brief instant I made out a distant dome light, coming on inside of his car. The car door slammed and the light went out, but before it did I thought I might have gotten the impression of hair pulled into a ponytail. The engine fired, tires ground into gravel and the car drove off without turning on its lights, leaving me behind. I stood trying to listen for its direction, but soon the car drove too far away.

A FEW MINUTES later I walked into the police spotlight with my hands raised. Several cars had arrived, including an ambulance. Radios squawked, and blue lights flashed. My car parked behind the squad cars.

"What happened?" shouted Detective Andrews.

I sank down on the wet sidewalk to catch my breath. Andrews and someone else crossed in front of the spotlight. Rain splattered and dripped off of their Stetsons.

"Drove off," I said between deep breaths. "Couldn't see the car. Into that back neighborhood, couldn't get there in time."

Andrews repeated the report into his shoulder radio. Deputy Burnette sat in my car, holding and talking to Kix. Mental note to send her flowers. Emily Newman stood near the ambulance with a poncho wrapped around her shoulders, talking to someone in a rain jacket. Pretty good response time, considering I only made the call ten minutes ago.

"I could be wrong, but I think..." I said, and I blew rainwater out of my mouth, "our shooter might be a woman."

46

I lay in bed that night, jumping at shadows. Mackenzie August, Super Wimp.

I'd discovered a dead body, been the chief suspect in a homicide investigation, and been shot at. Six times, one of which had put a hole an inch above the bumper of my car. All in a good day's work as a South Hill Middle School teacher.

The next day I was still exhausted. Sheriff's office was checking bullet casings for prints. A deputy found a partial tire track and taken a picture before the rain washed away the evidence. Maybe they'd learned something new from banging on doors in the neighborhood behind the school. I was intentionally not calling to find out. Kix and I wanted to think about something else, so we played Halo while it rained outside. Then we played with blocks. Then we practiced crawling. Then we took a nap. Mine was cut short by nightmare gunfire, hitting my mother, hitting my former partner, hitting me, hitting my son. I took a shower to wash away the dream.

Keep it together, Dad, Kix told me.

My phone rang around four o'clock.

"Hey stranger."

"Hey Taylor," I said. She was poison. Ill tempered, crass, and back-stabbing. But my heart quickened at the sound of her voice.

If the obsession theory was true then Taylor jumped to my top suspect. Especially because the killer had a ponytail.

"Ever heard of Affair on the Square?" she asked.

"Is that a movie?"

"No, stupid. It's a shindig. It's fun. You can meet me there, down-town South Hill tonight. The rain is supposed to let up, darlin', but they have big tents just in case. Beer, games, music, me. What else do you need?"

A bulletproof vest?

"Sure," I said. "Why not."

Sergeant Bingham called and I put it on speaker. He asked, "How's it feel to have a stalker?"

"Very gratifying. A lot of hard work paying off." Kix and I were cruising away from our house toward South Hill.

"I'm just surprised you only have one."

"I'm glad you said that," I said. "I felt like someone should."

"How sure are you the South Hill shooter is your stalker?"

I blew some air out of my mouth, and thought for a second.

"Kinda sure," I said. "The profile for the shooter is bizarre. White female, careful, pragmatic, obsessed, educated, leaves notes, and good with computers. Also a killer."

"Did you say female?"

"Yup. She made an attempt on another employee last night. I chased her away but couldn't catch her."

"Couldn't catch her," he repeated.

"Stop smiling. And she can impersonate the sheriff."

"Weird," he said.

"She lured another staff member to the school, pretending to be the sheriff on the phone. But she's not a great shot."

"You still getting shot at?"

"Professional hazard," I said.

"Of a teacher?"

"A really mean and scary teacher. Why'd you call me?" I asked.

"Anne made me. I think she's jealous of the stalker. Keep us posted."

THE AFFAIR on the Square celebrated fall in a parking lot near the library. Lanterns, pumpkins, bales of hay, and scarecrows mixed in among the stage, snack tables, beer venders, ring toss, bean bag toss, bobbing for apples, and other games. Hundreds of people had shown up. A bluegrass band played on stage. I'd stopped to pick up Stephen along the way, and parked three blocks from the library. I was pretty sure Taylor wasn't going to be overly excited about having one of our eighth-grade students tag along with us, but I figured Stephen needed someone to bring him since his mom worked nights. I also knew that having Stephen there would keep me from making out with Taylor again, which I definitely did not want to let myself do. And, since Taylor had climbed to the top of my suspect list, having another witness around would help reduce the chances of being shot. The streets were damp and the sky threatened, but for the moment we were dry.

Taylor called and hurried to greet us. She reached out to take Kix, which made both him and me very nervous, but he went anyway. She cooed and tickled him until he warmed up to her. I knew the feeling. She made a thin sweater and jeans look good. "Hi there, stud."

"Hi there, killer."

"Killer? New nickname? I like it."

She led us deeper into the crowd. Stephen saw friends and disappeared. I spotted a candied apple covered with chocolate chips that had my name on it.

"So." Taylor beamed. "I was arrested."

"You must have a great lawyer."

"Not really arrested, you know. Just questioned."

"What about?"

"The murder," she said, and she reached out to hold my hand before I was ready. "I told them that you'd vouch for me." Her hand felt warm and she kept a steady pressure.

"Is that so."

"Yes indeed. Jesus, look at all the stares we're getting. Wow, we must look great together."

"You and Roy were close, right? How are you doing with his death?"

"I'm fine. I mean, you know, I cried and everything. But I'm fine," she said, and she bounced Kix and tickled him some more. "You want a beer? I've already had one."

"Nah, I'm good. I can't vouch for you, Taylor. We weren't together when Roy was murdered."

"I know, but you can tell them you know it wasn't me. His wife told the police Roy was going to meet me that night, which is just nonsense, but you can tell them I'm not a murderer."

"If it worked like that," I said, "you could just get Detective Andrews to vouch for you."

She whipped her head around to look up at me through her lashes, some of her hair coming to rest across her cheek.

"Why, handsome, are you jealous?"

"Yup. I really wish I could get my hair like his."

"Where did you hear about me and Detective Andrews?" she asked.

"It's a small town."

"Well. Don't worry. He wasn't man enough for me. He's just an attractive place to visit now and then. No need to be jealous, Mr. August."

"I'll keep that in mind," I said.

"Besides, you're famous. Famous people don't get jealous."

"I didn't realize I'm famous."

"Oh yes. Can't you see everyone looking at you? You made the paper for the fourth time today."

"Really *really* small town."

"This time there's a big write-up with your photo and everything. In the picture, you're sitting in the rain, talking with the police. It's very debonair."

"Sure is, asshole," Jon Murphy said. Jon Murphy the drug dealer. He sauntered up, the same girlfriend in tow. He wore new running shoes, dark-washed designer jeans and an expensive-looking pullover rain jacket. She wore the same shoes and top last time I saw her. How embarrassing. "It's all very debonair."

"Jon. What's it like to be out on bail? Does it tingle all over?"

"Funny guy. Look, babe, look how funny he is."

I looked at babe and said, "I am pretty funny, you know."

"Hey Williams, how you doing, sweetie," he said.

"Hello," she replied coolly. "Don't make trouble, Jonathan."

"Why not." He chuckled. "You still packing heat?"

"No. Pig. Are you?"

Standing there listening to a drug dealer talk about guns with a woman I suspected of murder, who happened to be holding my son and my hand, I decided my life had gotten weird enough that I needed to check into children-sized bulletproof vests too. And maybe a child-sized shoulder rig and pistol.

The South makes people go crazy about guns.

"Your girl smooth pulled a gun on me, hero," Jon said. "Couple years ago."

"At least you know what 'No' means now," Taylor said. "I did 'babe' a favor."

"Doesn't stop her doing *favors* for me, sweetie," Jon said, and babe crossed her arms uncomfortably. Poor babe, this was awkward. "Williams and I used to go out." He winked at me. No surprise. I assumed every guy had been out with Taylor until they proved otherwise.

"Two dates," Taylor said. "That's it."

"Don't need a gun now, sweetie. You've got the Fighting Father," he said.

"The what?"

"The Fighting Father," Taylor said. "You really need to start reading the paper."

"What's a matter," Jon said. "Can't read, hero?"

"No. Hey, do you have any pot on you? I'm all out."

His smile disappeared and he walked into the crowd, his girl following. I watched him leave and sighed.

"That was rude," I said. "Should I apologize?"

"What?" Taylor snapped. "Are you kidding? That guy is scum."

"But I'm not," I said. And then I noticed that most of the people around actually were watching us.

"See?" she said sweetly.

I got my hands on that candied apple and followed Taylor around because she would not let go of Kix. She took pictures of him sitting next to a jack-o-lantern, and of both of them posing beside a scarecrow.

Mr. Charlie spotted me and patted me on the back. Taylor and Kix were making faces at the scarecrow. Mr. Charlie held a rolled-up newspaper in his hand. I took it from him. "I thought you might want to see this."

The picture was just like Taylor described. Someone with a camera had been there when I was sitting in the police spotlight, talking with Andrews. The article mentioned me discovering the two bodies, helping bust Murphy, briefly being considered a suspect, and saving Emily Newman. Her account of the ordeal sounded harrowing, and I came off rather heroic. Someone at the paper had done their research. They discovered I used to be a cop and then worked at a church. And now, apparently, I was the Fighting Father. Ugh.

The story was told from Emily's point of view. I'd been unavailable for comment. Darn right. The press still didn't know the murderer was good with computers and sending fake emails, which was good.

"Dang," I said.

"What?"

"It looks like I've put on weight," I said.

"The Fighting Father," Mr. Charlie said. "It's a little disrespectful, Mr. August. How long have you been ordained?"

"I'm not. And I'm not Catholic, so I'm not a Father."

"What are you?" he asked.

"Dunno. I'm not a fighter, either."

"That's not what the RO says," he chuckled.

"He told people?" I asked. "About our fight?"

"Yessir. He told everyone you two slugged it out, that's how he hurt his hand."

"I'm glad that didn't end up in the paper," I said. "I'd be the Fighting Cop Puncher."

"So it's true?"

"A little," I said, and handed the paper back.

"Listen, Mr. August," he said, in that great, slow drawl of his. "I hope I didn't get you into much trouble, about the email. I didn't know you thought I had sent you an email, so when I told the police, I know they assumed...that you were the..."

"Someone has been sending bogus emails. Not your fault."

"They brought me in for questioning yesterday. I don't have a good alibi, but I would never kill Mackenzie, or Roy."

"Oh yeah? You're not a coldblooded killer?"

"No, sir. If I was, I wouldn't admit it to the Fighting Father."

"Don't call me that."

Stephen showed up, holding Kix. He looked at me questioningly. I turned and saw Taylor buying another beer and talking on the phone.

"Thanks," I told him and took my son.

"Everybody's bummed," Stephen noted.

"Yes, these events are usually more lively," Mr. Charlie agreed, looking around. "The murders are the biggest thing to happen to South Hill in years. How you doing, Stephen?"

"Good. Think we'll have school tomorrow?"

"Mmhm, I think so," he said.

"Mr. August, some kids are calling you the Fighting Father."

"I heard."

"Matthew says his mom won't let him come to school, because she thinks you're the killer."

"Matthew's mom sucks."

"Whoa."

"Don't tell anyone I said that. The killer rumor might help with my classroom management skills."

Mr. Charlie thought that was hilarious. He was correct.

Kristen and Curtis found me soon. I hadn't seen Curtis since I ate dinner at their house. They were holding hands. I wanted to hold hands with someone. Who wasn't a murderer. "Hey there, hero," Kristen said, and she punched me in the arm. "Or should I say Fighting Father?"

"I'm Protestant."

"Fighting Pastor doesn't have the same ring," she said.

"Protestant Pugilist," Curtis offered.

"Nice. Kept the alliteration," I said. "Kristen, that's where several words in a row begin with the same letter."

"I know, jerk. Hi, Kix!"

Kix approved.

Curtis said, "I saw the news last night. There's a shot of you driving away from the crime scene. Taped it, if you want to watch."

"I thought I got away before the vans got their cameras out."

"Apparently not. Kristen was over near the school last night," Curtis said. "Give her a call next time and she'll come help out."

Kristen snorted a laugh. "Help with a shootout."

"What were you doing there?" I asked.

"Nothing. On my way back from visiting friends."

I nodded.

Kix shot me a look - *she's the killer!*

I shot him a look back - *no she's not!*

"Where's your daughter?" I asked.

"With her grandparents. She's crawling now, did I tell you?"

"No," I said. "How super for you. You're obviously superior parents and one day your child will be my child's boss."

"Naw, don't say that," Cannon said, walking up behind me. He wore a baseball cap over his long, shaggy hair. He patted me on the back. "Kix is a fine baby, real nice boy."

"This is like the teachers' work room," I said, and I shook his hand. He had a mean grip and used it on me often. Kix pointed at Mr. Cannon and called him a name. "We're all here."

"I called you, left a message on your machine," Cannon said.

"About church?"

"About this, the Affair in the Square. It's usually a real nice time. Thought I'd offer to buy you a beer."

"Thanks, but I'm on my way out."

"Okay. Stay here. I'll be right back."

Kix and I ignored Cannon's advice and we strolled through the Affair. Much of the crowd watched us. No one approached or spoke, just stared a little too long. Surrounded by so many people who knew me, I felt alone.

I collected Stephen and started for the car, but resource Officer Steve Reed stopped me. He wore his tight belt and over-flowing khaki uniform. "Hey boy. Deputy Andrews got a hit on his background checks," he said. "Mr. Gee has a prior."

"Mr. Gee? The custodian?"

"That's him."

"He's not the shooter," I said.

"What? He cleans your classroom. The tires look the same."

"It's not him. I might not be able to tell who the shooter is, but I can tell who it's not. And its not him. What's his prior? Assault?"

"Domestic disturbance."

"It's not him. Tell Andrews to keep looking."

Reed walked off unhappily. I wondered how many people he'd already told that Mr. Gee was the killer.

Time to go. Too many people here.

I finished strapping Kix into his car seat and Taylor appeared behind me. Like a ghost. She smiled halfheartedly and didn't speak until Stephen had climbed into the passenger seat and closed the door.

"Leaving?"

"I don't know if we're in the festive mood."

"I get it, you know," she said. She held what I guessed was her third or fourth beer. Her words weren't slurred, but they weren't stable either. "I understand."

"Tell me what you understand."

"You, me, us," she said. "Why you won't date me."

"Why?"

"It's because I'm not good enough."

"I never said that," I said. "Nor have I even thought that." Which was true. But if she was the shooter, then I'd think that a lot.

"I didn't say you did, Mack. I said I'm not good enough. You're a good person. You are. I get it. You're trying to be. An' I'm not. We're kind of the same, 'cept you're trying and I'm not."

"I am trying."

"We're both young, we're both good-looking, people want to be with us...but you're a pastor."

"No I'm not."

"You're a pastor," she said again, "and you're the kind who doesn't fuck around. That's important to you. I get it. You're trying, but if you're with me then you'd have to stop. Stop trying."

"It has a lot less to do with you and a lot more to do with me. If I dated *anybody* then I'd fail. I don't trust myself. I'd fail you and I'd fail me, and I'm tired of failing. I want my next one to work. And I'm not ready for it yet."

"Why does it have to work? Why can't it just be fun?"

"Casual is a lie sold by commercials. I tried it. Ask yourself something. Why are you so eager to date me? I'm not worth the effort. You barely know me. You've dated everyone I've met here, and you're still looking. Maybe in a few years you'll be like me and be sick of failing."

Talking with a murder suspect about romance felt odd.

She crossed her arms, stared at me with eyes that were mostly dry, and spun to walk back to the Affair on the Square.

"You need a ride home?" I called.

She didn't answer.

47

My alarm clock showed 12:30. In the middle of the night. The house stood silent and dark, except for my table lamp. Rain pattered intermittently on the window. I couldn't get to sleep so I lay in bed reading Donald Miller's new book. I think we'd be friends, or at least he'd understand my uncertainty towards churches.

He had just convicted me about giving some of my money away when the power went out.

Third power outage since we moved here. Our sparsely populated lake community was powered by lines that ran through miles of forest, and the wind liked to throw tree branches at the lines. I rolled out of bed and peered out of the closed blinds.

The streetlight still burned. And I could make out the faint wet glow of my distant neighbor's porch lights. It was only our house then, and our electric bill was paid and we certainly hadn't blown a fuse. Our power outage was almost certainly not the result of natural causes.

Which meant we had an unwelcome guest downstairs. My chest turned icy.

The breaker box was located in the garage, directly under my bedroom, so I either forgot to close the garage door or the intruder had been quiet forcing his or her way in. I guess it didn't really matter one way or the other.

My pistol was still in its holster on the dresser. I pulled it out, creating the distinctive sound of the metal sliding against the leather, and pushed the safety off. I'd left my cell in the car and unplugged the house phone. Brilliant.

Standing at the bedroom door, I paused to evaluate. Things had changed. No longer was this only a murder investigation, this had become personal. No longer was I a careless cop, I was a father. The job lost its place as top priority, and Kix's safety was paramount. That meant I had to fight in a different way. My responsibilities required me to catch the shooter, but not at the expense of Kix. It felt like boxing with one arm tied behind my back.

The person downstairs was the shooter I'd been looking for. I knew it. Had to be. I highly doubted Steve and his two drunk friends would be looking for another fight on this cold, rainy night. And I could think of no other reason why an intruder would go to all the trouble of shutting down the power in a single house with almost no neighbors around for miles in any direction. Anne the criminal psychologist had guessed right; I had a stalker. As a detective, I'd seen this happen before. The question was what was the shooter doing here? Stalkers dealing with obsession often end up destroying the object of their obsession. Which in this case, was me. Was that the reason someone prowled my house? Something more innocent? Something more sinister?

First priority, Kix stayed alive. Two ways into his room: his bedroom door, which was directly across the hallway from my bedroom door, and his ground-level window. I couldn't cover the window from the stairwell, which is where I would have a tactical advantage. The only place I could cover both window and door was from inside of his room. That would help me with my second priority, keeping myself alive, but inhibit my third, catching the stalker.

I made it to the wall in his room without the floor squeaking and sunk to the carpet, my back resting against the wood paneling.

From here I could look straight out of his bedroom door, into the hall, and into my bedroom. I could also see out his locked window, which let in a small amount of moonlight. Other than that, I couldn't see much. My eyes were still used to the light from my table lamp.

The house held the stark quiet of midnight. Eerily silent. The intruder was going to have a hard time navigating in the dark. I would be able to hear the person coming, and as soon as I saw a head poke around the bedroom door I was going to blow it off. The living room clock sounded impossibly loud.

A rustle from the stairwell. I kept plastic bags of dirty diapers there at night. My stalker had either stepped on one accidentally or moved it out of the way.

The intruder had to assume we were both asleep. It was after midnight and all the lights had been off for over an hour, except my table lamp which probably didn't show through the blinds. A little noise wasn't that terrible, considering both Kix and I were asleep. Or so she thought.

I assumed it was a she. I'd never seen the shooter except vaguely, but I knew she was thin and had long enough hair to wear a ponytail. I think. I rubbed my eyes and forced myself to concentrate on the moment, even though I was tired of waiting.

One of the stairs squeaked. I had been listening for that, because they always squeaked for me. The squeak sounded near the top of the staircase, which meant other stairs hadn't squeaked. So she probably weighed significantly less than me, another reason to assume a girl.

The ice in the refrigerator shifted noisily, maybe starting to melt. I imagined the stalker at the top of the stairs, peering around before entering the hallway, being startled by the sound.

The minutes kept dragging slowly by. She was patient. I bet the time had moved to well after one in the morning. My eyes were nearly adjusted to the dark. I could see everything I needed to.

Was she carrying her gun in her hand? A knife? Wearing a mask? Certainly gloves. In her socks, probably. Shoes would be wet. I had to resist the impulse to take deep breaths or fidget. I also had to keep talking myself out of rushing the hall, getting it over with.

Kix grunted and rolled over, disquieting me. If the shooter was observant, she might start to wonder why she hadn't heard similar noises from my bedroom. Did she know which room was mine? Was she here for Kix? I tightened my grip on the gun.

A soft footfall in the hall and then rustling in the kitchen. Did she mean to go to the kitchen?

A new thought occurred to me. Had she been here before? Was this a regular routine? Were the previous power outages not really caused by the wind? Maybe she'd been here before, and planned to simply leave after snooping around. If it sounded like she was turning around and heading for the exit, then I could leave the bedroom and catch her going back down the stairs. If she did this regularly then she might not even be armed. Possibilities flew through my mind.

More footsteps in the hallway, the soft sound of carpet being compressed. Toward the bedrooms. Both doors were open, which would she choose? I held the pistol in my right hand, arm straight, elbow resting on my bent, supportive knee, barrel aimed at the right edge of the door.

The movement stopped just before it reached the open doorway. I could see straight into my bedroom and I could also see a very thin section of the opposite hall wall. My eyes were constantly moving, not letting them settle and become blurry, using my peripheral sensitivity. I was ready to shoot high if she was standing or low if she crouched. A fine sheet of rain washed across the outside of Kix's bedroom window.

More waiting. The killer might not know which room was which, and might be inching forward, inspecting the rooms as they slowly came into view. By leaning right she'd be able to see more of Kix's bedroom, and by leaning left the angle would let her see more of my room. She would see my bed. Would the ruffled sheets and comforter look occupied? Kix's crib was on the far wall, and would be one of the first things she'd see.

Every few minutes I could hear her shift slightly. We were only ten feet apart. I'd still seen no movement, which meant she still hadn't seen either of the rooms fully.

Kix whimpered in his sleep and I instinctively tensed. Outside an owl hooted. My butt had grown sore. I was sick of waiting.

A new thought occurred to me and with it came an increasing awareness of its accuracy; the shooter might have guessed the situation. Depending on how far she'd crept forward and peered into the room, she might have seen that my bed was empty. I became more anxious with that thought. And the longer she waited, the greater the chances she would figure out I knew that she knew.

She knew I waited for her. And I knew that she knew. And soon she would realize that I knew she knew.

We had an uneasy, unspoken but shared stalemate.

My eyes started to see things, flashes of black by the door. I grew jumpy, my nerves on edge, wondering if she would stick her gun around the door and start firing. But she couldn't be sure which room I was in. I envisioned her slowly leaning her head into view, her one eye beyond the doorframe widening as she saw me, my eyes widening in recognition, my gun firing, blood painting the wall and carpet behind her.

The person in the hallway became less quiet. I could hear her move, fidget, take deep breaths. I kept as quiet as possible so she wouldn't know which room I was in.

The waiting continued and I remained sharp, just in case she was inching forward. I pressed my thumb against the hammer of my gun until it hurt. Maybe I should pull the hammer back, loudly cocking the gun. The noise would reveal which room I hid in, but would let her know death waited inside.

The choice was taken from me. In a flurry of movement that sounded impossibly loud after the silence, she rushed. I got further behind my gun, looking along the sight, ready to kill, but the footsteps pounded away from me and thundered down the steps. Downstairs I heard two doors crash open, and then nothing. I was tempted to look out the window but if she had a gun then I'd be an easier target for her to shoot than she would be for me. The odds weren't worth it. Tonight a stalemate was okay. Kix and I were both alive and when morning arrived we'd still be.

I still sat in the same position when the sun began to come through the windows hours later.

———————

48

D eputy Andrews and I stood with our arms crossed, looking at the door to the garage. It stood wide open with no signs of being forced.

"Think you locked it?" he asked.

"Yup."

"Which means they probably got a key," he said.

"Yuck."

"That's not fun to think about."

"No," I said. "No it isn't."

I had called Deputy Andrews at six to come look over the house and see if I'd missed anything. The intruder had obviously entered through the garage. There were still small damp places from the rain, and a faint muddy footprint. A collection of wet mud marked where she'd most likely taken off her boots. No prints on any doorknobs, which meant she'd been opening doors with a rag and wiped mine off too. Nothing in the kitchen was disturbed, and there was a faint depression in the hallway carpet where she had stood, silently waiting during our stalemate. She'd gotten real close to my doorway.

He finished his inspection and joined me in the kitchen. I ate

Cheerios and I poured him a bowl. We chewed without talking for a while.

"Thing is," I said, "last night would have been easy, if I wasn't a dad. I could have hidden anywhere and taken her. But that small, tiny chance of me getting hurt and Kix being defenseless...that changes everything." I poured us both a glass of orange juice. "I've been in much worse spots than last night. No problem. But with my son in the house..." I shook my head.

"You're a good father," he said.

"No, but I hope to be one day. Most guys have nine months to prepare. I had zero."

"Look," he said. "Is it Taylor? We've gotten several calls from LA, saying you can smell lies, you always know who did what just by looking at them. If you think it's Taylor then we'll bring her in again, grill her for a few hours, see if she cracks."

"I don't know," I said. "She's the only one who makes sense, and she's been pretty aggressive. But I spend a lot of time with her at work, and she's acted flippant, careless about the murders. Not proud or guilty."

"You're the first guy's ever told her no," he said.

"Allen was dead before I told her no," I said.

"Was she chasing you before he died?"

"Yeah. I'd already decided she wasn't right for me. She maybe could've picked up on that. But even so, that's a pretty thin motive for shooting someone in the forehead."

"She knew and flirted with both victims," he said. "You spent time with both victims. The notes left were written by someone educated. She sounds like she's been obsessed with you since you met."

"All good points."

He finished his juice, set the glass down and said, "Going to work today?"

"Yes," I said. "My last day."

"You're quitting?"

"I think so. I don't know what else to do. We're sitting ducks, and Kix is too valuable," I said, frustrated.

"You'd be missed."

"Not worth the risk."

"You could ship Kix off to your father's," he suggested.

"I don't ship Kix anywhere."

"Sorry."

"I don't know what to do." I laced my fingers behind my head and paced the kitchen. "I promised Ms. Allen I'd find the killer. I promised Mr. Charlie too."

"We'll find him. Or her."

"Probably. But that's beside the point. I don't want to quit, to let them down, make myself a liar."

"You barely know them."

"That's not the point either," I said. "What am I, if I'm not hard working, determined, honest? A quitter? Besides, I used to be great at this. About a year ago I was one of the best in LA. I gotta figure out how to balance honor, duty, loyalty, commitment, and fatherhood. But I can't sit around here until I do. The intruder last night might have been headed into Kix's room instead of mine."

"That's a scary thought."

"You're catching on."

He nodded and said, "See you at school."

THE MAYOR, the sheriff, and the superintendent all made speeches on the news. The mayor did his best to look comforting and in control and as though he was personally doing his best to catch the killer. Sheriff Mitchell promised that there would be several deputies on school grounds during the day and they would close off the campus at night. Everyone would be perfectly safe and had nothing to fear by going to school. Superintendent Neal stressed the importance of going to school, pledged more security would keep everyone safe, and stated that he would personally be walking the halls of South Hill Middle. So when I arrived at school I wasn't surprised to see three squad cars in addition to Officer Reed's car in front, as well as a handful of news vans. Hopefully none of the cameras would zero in on me and notice my car was stuffed with most of our belongings.

I wore a zip-up rain jacket so I could hide my shoulder rig. Principal Martin would have to come wrestle me herself if she wanted me to go without my gun today.

A little under three fourths of the students in my classes showed up. The braver ones raised their hands and asked me if I was the Fighting Father, was it scary being shot at, and did I know that Jimmy's mom wouldn't let him come to school because of me.

When my planning period rolled around I went straight to the principal's office. Ms. Martin's door was open. She sat behind her desk with her hands crossed. She wore a brown, fine houndstooth suit with an open white collar. Her hair was back in a bun.

"Expecting me?"

"A little," she replied.

"I quit."

She allowed herself a small smile. Rare for her.

"I have a flair for the dramatic," I said.

"I noticed.

"Today is my last day."

"Detective Andrews is here. Rumors are circulating."

"The rumor about an intruder being at my house is true. If it was just me at home then no problem. But it's me and a nine-month-old, and apparently it's personal. I can't stay in town anymore."

"Where will you go?"

"Roanoke, three hours west from here," I said.

"And do what?"

"Not sure. I didn't sleep last night, so I'm not thinking clearly. Perhaps I'll arrange for childcare and come back for the killer."

"Would you come back if we catch the killer for you?"

"Wow," I said, and I rubbed my forehead. "That makes me sound like such a..."

"Weenie?"

"Yes. A weenie."

"No one thinks of you as such. Many of my teachers are out 'sick' or taking personal days. I had to call in all of my subs."

"The fast-paced life of a principal."

"Have you thought about having the police patrol your house?" she asked.

"That would be a short-term solution. The killer needs to be caught. If I leave and someone around here starts going missing, or someone shows up in Roanoke, then we'll know exactly who we're looking for."

"Do you have any guesses?" she asked.

"Yes."

"Is it one of our staff?" she asked.

"Yes."

"Shit," she said and looked down at her hands, which looked like they might be shaking if they let go of each other. "Isn't that enough to arrest them?"

"Both the sheriff and Investigator Andrews know. But it's not enough."

"Will you tell me?"

"No. You'd act differently around the person and they'd know."

"Mr. August," she said, her voice shaky. "I'm a single parent too. What am I supposed to do? I can't run away."

We sat in silence for a long time, me searching for an answer. Eventually she got up and went to her personal bathroom. I left and went straight to Mr. Suhr.

"I don't know how to do this," I told him. He wore work khakis spotted with paint and a plaid shirt with the sleeves rolled up, and monitored a very small classroom, nailing together what looked like shelves.

"Do what, Mr. August?"

"I don't know how to do the right thing. I don't even know what the right thing is. For the sake of my family, I think I should leave. Make this my last day. But what about everyone else?"

"What about everyone else?"

"They're my neighbors, right? I know I'm supposed to be a good neighbor, look not only to my own interests. I know I'm supposed to take care of widows and orphans. I know that to whom much is given much is required. But it's my kid," I said. "If Kix dies, I will too. I've lost too many people, I'm barely hanging on as it is."

"The Lord is with you, Mr. August," he said.

"I don't know what the hell that means. Is He with me even if I run away?"

"Even if you take your family to safety."

"And if I stay?"

"Even if you stay to bring safety to other families."

"You're a fat load of help."

He smiled.

"But you are comforting."

"God does not usually tell us right or left," he said slowly. "Instead, He tells us right or wrong. I do not know if your question has a wrong answer. Perhaps you have the freedom to choose either way and know that either way the Lord will be with you."

I left. That didn't help at all. I didn't understand Christians.

I SAT AT MY DESK, staring at my monitor. Trying to grade papers and failing.

Movement at the window. A camera disappeared from view. I went out the back door of my trailer, circled around front, and caught a cameraman by surprise. From a newspaper, most likely. Seedy-looking guy, greasy and fat. I took his camera and smashed it on the ground.

"Hey! That's destruction of my property!"

"No it's not. You dropped it."

I went back inside before I punched him. I was sick of being in the paper. I buzzed the office to alert the resource officer we had an intruder, and then I tried to grade papers. Five minutes later, Steven Reed opened the door. He kept his right hand on the knob and stood in the doorway.

"Found'em," he said. "I kicked him off campus. Said you broke his camera?"

"He dropped it. Wink."

"You might make the front page again, if he was able to salvage the memory stick."

"At least I wore my nice socks today."

"Also, Mr. August," he said. "I quit the pot."

"Oh yeah?"

"Yeah. Not a hit since our...argument."

"Hang in there. It gets easier with time."

"I told Jon not to come around anymore."

"Poor Jon Murphy," I said.

"Yeah. Poor Jon."

He stood there awkwardly for a long moment, looking like he wanted to say something else but couldn't find the words. Finally he nodded at me, turned around and walked out. I could be wrong, but I took the head nod as a *Thank You.*

You're welcome, Officer Reed. For hitting you in the jaw. I take all the credit.

I couldn't leave. What was wrong with me. All that's necessary for the triumph of evil, and that kinda inspirational stuff. If Officer Reed could take a stand, then I could too. Because no way he was tougher than me. I was the toughest. And the good-lookingest. And tough good-looking people such as myself didn't let the government handle our problems. What was the difference between Detective Andrews and myself? Other than his great hair? He got paid to catch killers and I didn't? So what?

I couldn't spend another night at the lake house, even with a patrol car making passes in front of my house. Not with Kix in danger. I'd need to leave him with James and Leta, or....or something. I didn't know. But I couldn't leave.

The administrators called the grades one at a time into the gym for separate assemblies. Normally rowdy and nearly uncontrollable en masse, the eighth graders were silent today.

Principal Martin and one of the guidance counselors did the talking, making the collective grief and fear audible and more bearable. Martin gave a few brief details about Emily Newman, the resource teacher who had heroically shown up for work today, and her close call at the school just two nights ago. It had been a long two days. The counselor gave them permission to feel afraid and the freedom to cry. The sadness and comfort was unifying. I felt better too, despite everyone sneaking glances at me. Before we left, Principal Martin announced that all after-school activities had been cancelled and that police were going to swing by the school once an hour and arrest anyone they found.

I stayed in my trailer and did my best to concentrate and finish grading papers for an hour after school. Mr. Charlie, Mr. Suhr, Ms. Friedmond, Mrs. Short, and Mr. Cannon came to check on me and cheer me up.

On my way out, I passed Principal Martin.

"See you tomorrow," I said, not breaking stride.

She let out a breath which sounded like she'd been holding an hour. I took that as a good sign. Climbing into my car, I phoned Sergeant Bingham on his cell.

"Saw you on cable news," he said. "The Fighting Father sounds stupid."

"I had an intruder last night," I said. "I scared them off. Because I'm a hero."

"Fuck. This thing is getting too real."

"I can't run. I came close, but I'm staying. Gotta see this one through. The whole town is spooked."

"I'll be on the first flight tomorrow," he said. "One of us can be with Kix every hour of the day."

"You got vacation time?"

"Months. But we'll only need a few days."

"I appreciate it."

"August," he said. "This doesn't mean we're friends. Just stay alive until tomorrow night."

"Yes sir."

49

T he sheriff was out when I got to the station. Andrews stood at his desk with a mug of coffee in his fist.

"I'm staying," I said. "Fill me in."

Three nights in a row the killer had been active. First night, Roy. Second night, Emily Newman. Third night, me. That was a lot of alibis to check. The custodian, Mr. Gee, had no alibi for the previous two nights and his tires might or might not match the picture of the tire tracks left at the crime scene outside of the school. Mr. Charlie also had no firm alibi for the previous two nights but he had digital timestamps on emails sent during the Emily-Newman-fiasco. He would've had time to get home and send the emails after the shooting, but not much. Taylor Williams had so far refused to cooperate, declaring herself immune because of me and Andrews. The owners of the guest house she lived in had been gone for weeks.

Everything coming back from Roy's murder matched Allen's. Same gun, no signs of struggle, nothing weird on credit card or cell phone receipts. Clean, except for the email he'd received from Charlie about meeting him and Williams at school. That told us nothing new. The school's central office was researching how the emails could be sent other than password sharing, which Charlie denied. The fake phone call to Emily Newman came from a payphone only a few miles from the school. No prints, no witnesses.

Deputies were banging on doors, including Murphy's and other usual suspects. The media phoned regularly.

"I need you to bring Taylor in," I said. "Tonight. Grill her."

"Okay. We planned on tomorrow morning but tonight works. Why?"

"So I know where she is and where she isn't."

"Planning on breaking into her place?" he asked.

"Not telling."

"Deniability?" he asked.

"Andrews. Stop saying things out loud we have to deny later. What the hell is wrong with you."

"Give us," he said, and glanced at his watch. "An hour and a half. Then you'll be free for several after that."

Tonight I would visit the bedroom of Taylor Williams.

But it wouldn't be much fun.

I walked out to my car. Darkness had fallen and the rain returned. It was an overcast dreary kinda day. I drove down Highway 58 to Leta's house in silence. Hopefully I could talk her into watching my son a few more hours, and then Kix and I would get a hotel. I drove with no radio, no podcasts. Only the rain and my thoughts.

I pulled into Leta's and killed the engine. The gravel crunched wetly under my shoes and the rain made spots on my pressed red shirt. I loosened my tie. The trusty Honda was clicking and hot in the cold fall air. Floorboards squeaked as I ascended the porch. Leta met me at the top. She wore the white apron with pink flowers that she loved so much. Her hands held worried fistfuls of the fabric.

"You told me not to let Kix out of my sight unless you or the sheriff called." Her voice was shaking.

"Right," I said, and the hairs on the back of my neck stood up.

"Well, he called."

"The sheriff? What'd he say?"

"He said one of the teachers would come by for Kix. He said you were in trouble."

"That wasn't the sheriff."

"I see that," she cried. "I'm so sorry."

"Is Kix gone?"

"Yes."

"Which teacher?"

She held back a sob.

"Which teacher came and got Kix?" I repeated, my palms starting to sweat.

"I don't know."

"What'd she look like?"

"He. He was tall and skinny. Long shaggy hair."

I hit the ground running, kicking up gravel.

50

Puzzle pieces crashed into place. Cannon. Cannon had been very interested in my life ever since I'd met him. Cannon was thin and had long hair which he pulled into a ponytail. Cannon lived a few miles from the school and he was also a computer whiz. Taylor hadn't disguised her voice to sound like the sheriff; Cannon had.

But Cannon was a Baptist. A devout one. Baptists can't kill people. They can't even drink.

My heart beat so hard that the steering wheel shifted under my fists. Was Kix already dead? If so, Cannon would die too. And then most likely me. My son had been in the backseat, waving and singing earlier this morning. I could see his empty carseat in the rearview mirror. His diaper bag was stuffed full of wipes and toys and lying on the passenger seat beside me.

I pressed my foot all the way to the floor and got the car over ninety-five. My left hand flashed my high beams and my right pressed the horn anytime I saw oncoming traffic. Makeshift emergency lights and siren. Wipers churning full speed, throwing aside rain.

The police would be no help. I didn't want a hostage situation. If

Kix was alive then I'd take him back. If not, I'd kill Cannon. I might anyway. My tie lay on the floor because I couldn't breathe. Sweat and tears mixed in my eyes. The pounding raindrops began to take the shape of dead faces.

Please God. Not Kix.

I turned onto Highway 58, the car sliding through water across both lanes and into gravel on the far side before catching and powering forward. Cannon lived a little more than two miles past the school. I realized I'd been laying on the horn for the last thirty seconds and forced myself to let go.

I would pass the school before I got to his house. The campus lay just out of sight, five hundred yards away from the highway. I hated that school. I was so sick of being there at night. I almost passed it, but at the last second jammed on the brakes, cut the wheel and flew up the road, following a hunch.

I guessed right. Cannon stood at the school, in the rain underneath a streetlight which cast the front sidewalk in a sick, yellow glow. His car was parked in a handicapped spot. In his left arm he carried Kix.

My Accord slid to a stop beside his. Deep breath. Before getting out, I tore open the glove compartment and wrapped my left hand around the six-shot revolver. I still had the Kimber in my shoulder rig. I stood and started walking toward Cannon, keeping my left hand pinned against my left leg.

"I knew you'd come," Cannon said, softly enough so that I could barely hear him over the deluge. His white shirt was soaked, his long, stringy hair dripping, glasses foggy. "I knew you'd find me." My muscles were practically cramping with the desire to attack him, punch him until my knuckles split.

Kix wore the same jeans and long-sleeved T-shirt I'd dressed him in that morning. His shoes were missing. His eyelids were droopy and he was having trouble supporting his head. A long piece of silver duct tape had been wrapped around his head, covering his mouth. He drew breath only through his nose.

"What's wrong with him?"

"Nothing, he's fine," Cannon called through the rain. "He was upset, Mr. August, so I gave him something to make him sleepy. He's resting nicely now."

"What'd you give him?"

"Nothing lethal," he said, and he waved the question off with the gun in his right hand. A revolver. I hadn't seen the gun before because I'd been so focused on Kix. Water drops went flying as he waved it. I unzipped my jacket. "I knew you'd find me, Mr. August. I prayed you would."

"I prayed that too."

"You've come a long way, Mr. August. A long way. God is pleased."

"Maybe with one of us," I said. For the moment I was calm. Need crushed emotion. Focused adrenaline. Delayed aggression.

"You may not realize it yet," he said. "But God has big things planned for you."

"You sound like Mr. Suhr."

"Don't talk to me about that nigger. I'm sick of pretending his kind matter."

"Mr. Suhr never kidnapped my son."

"You of little faith." He smiled, the way I'd seen him smile for the last two months. Except now he carried a loaded gun and my son. "You aren't looking down, you aren't seeing your path. Your path brought you here, Mr. August. Your path brought you to me."

"Cannon, my path did not lead me here. You did," I said. His smile faltered briefly. "You murdered your coworkers. You broke into my classroom and my home. You stole and drugged my son."

"You know what I hate," he said, spitting out rain. "I hate weak-minded fools. Like the faggots who don't understand how God could condone violence in the Old Testament. Violence is necessary," he snapped and the insanity inside his head was briefly and clearly visible. "God used violence as a way to prune, to discipline, Mr. August. God disciplines His sons through pain. You needed pruning. Real powerful, holy pruning."

He set his right hand across Kix's stomach, the gun lying on my son's shirt. My Kimber was out in a flash.

"Get your gun away from him."

"Hey," he yelled, and flinched away from the barrel pointed at him. He hid behind Kix as best he could and pressed his revolver into Kix's neck. "No, no! Put your gun down. Mr. August! Put your gun down! This is not God's will."

I couldn't shoot him in the head. Not with his gun pressed so tightly against Kix, and not with his face hidden. I could hit him easily from the navel down, but he'd still be alive with a loaded weapon and a priceless hostage.

"Get your gun away from his neck."

"I see how upset you are, Mr. August. I understand. I know this is hard."

"Point your gun at me. Point it away from him."

"Haha, you see," he yelled. "Look at you! Your face is red. Don't you get it? You're blind. You've made your son an idol. You aren't able to do God's will. The burden you carry with you is too heavy."

"Point your gun at me and I'll stop pointing mine at you. Just don't point it at Kix."

"Fine." He smiled and turned his weapon on me. I took a deep breath, and aimed sideways at the school. Then I released the grip and let the pistol dangle from my trigger finger. "Are you happy, Mr. August? Are you satisfied with your false sense of security, of control?"

"Why'd you kill Mackenzie Allen? Why'd you kill Roy Davis?"

"I know you've read the Old Testament, Mr. August. You're a priest, for God's sake. And a real good one. You might not have known it, but you have become my spiritual mentor. How did God deal with the Israelites when they began to breed with the unclean, uncircumcised Philistines? Or the Moabites, those filthy, inbred enemies of God? How did God rebuke the Israelites? He disciplined them. He hurt them. God's people are holy, set apart. They do not sit in the seat of the scornful. Allen and Davis chose evil. Just like you, Mr. August. You chose evil. Evil friends. You walked in the way of the wicked. They had to die, for your sake, your future, to prune you."

"Why didn't you just tell me?"

"God is not in the earthquake!" he snarled. "Nor in the fire. God is in the whisper. You have to grow quiet and hear God for yourself. I removed distractions."

"You're not thinking clearly," I said. "Thou shall not murder."

"Those rules were for the Jews," he spit. "Those rules are tools to govern cattle, Mr. August. How many men did King David slaughter? Thousands. Those rules do not apply to kings, those rules do not apply to God's chosen, they do not apply to us."

"Why'd you kidnap Kix?" I needed to keep him talking while I looked for an advantage, an opening.

"Kix," he scoffed, and got a better grip on my son. They were both sopping wet, and Kix was heavy. Growing heavier and slipperier by the minute. "Your kid is the largest burden you carry, the largest distraction, the biggest golden calf of all. I called your former employers, Mr. August. You were a mighty weapon for God. A holy scythe. You jailed niggers, killed Latinos." As he spoke, water spit and drooled from his mouth onto the top of Kix's head.

"Called justice, Cannon."

"Then Kix was born. Your son, by a married woman. Did you not make the connection with Abraham? Do you not remember what happened to Abraham's first son? He was cast into the wilderness, Mr. August. Because of Abraham's lack of faith."

"Remove the tape, Cannon. He's having trouble breathing," I said. Kix was soaked, the rain falling directly on his face. His head rolled side to side. I deliberately stayed far enough away so that I couldn't hear him whimper. Otherwise I knew I'd start shooting. I had a gun in each hand.

"You think I would kill him before he's ready?"

"You've got my attention. Let him go," I said. My fist tightened on the hidden revolver pressed against my left hamstring. Water cascaded into my eyes.

"Think, Mr. August, think. Remember. Remember Abraham's other son. Remember Isaac and the test of faith."

My blood turned cold. I knew the story. God asked Abraham to sacrifice his only son, Isaac.

"It was a test, Cannon," I said. "Abraham didn't actually have to kill his son."

"You're right," he said, the barrel of his gun shaking. "He didn't. But he was willing."

"Well I'm not."

"Then your faith is too small. You don't pass the test."

"I don't care," I said.

"Samson was also a mighty weapon for God. But he allowed himself to become sidetracked by Delilah. What happened?"

"I don't care."

"You're not listening," he snapped. "You're better than this! I'm better than them! I need you. You need me. You need discipline and deliverance."

"Your faith is flawed, Cannon. My sin is between me and God. You have no part in it. You have taken it upon yourself to hand out judgment. What happens when people play God, Cannon?"

He stared at me in stony silence.

"What happens to people who play God?"

"You don't know," he said, growing angry. "You haven't been paying attention."

"What does the law hinge on, Cannon? Love."

"Do not question me," he snarled. "You disappoint, Mr. August. I expected you to be more receptive."

His voice had grown quiet, his face closed. He was going to shoot me. He'd already murdered two men at the school; I would be no different. I'd been shot before. I wasn't looking forward to it.

"You can't kill me, Cannon," I said.

"The Lord is my strength."

"I'm too far away and you're a bad shot. I'll dodge. And then I'm going to kill you."

"The Lord is my shield."

"Put Kix down and find out," I said, and I started pacing. He probably couldn't hit a moving target. I didn't know what else to do.

Cannon took the gun off of me and pointed it at Kix's temple.

"If you kill him," I said, "you're next."

"The Lord is my salvation."

"Not right now he's not, Cannon. And you know it. You kill my son, and I kill you. You and Kix will get to heaven at the same time. See how God feels about you then."

"You blaspheme," he said and he tried to get a better grip on Kix. He knew I was right. He had no element of surprise, and I was the better shot. We had a stalemate. I had no way of preventing him from killing Kix. But then he had no way of preventing me from killing him.

"You know I'm right," I said.

"The truth shall set you free."

"Set Kix free, Cannon. Set him down, put your gun down, I promise I won't kill you."

"I cannot. I still have a mission. A purpose."

Wheels spinning in his head. Inside of his madness he searched for an escape. A way out. A way to kill me. Even a madman possesses a scrap of self-preservation.

"You need help. Let me help you. If I'm your mentor then listen to me."

"Let us see, Mr. August," he said, slowly. "Let us see if God will let your son strike his heel upon the stone."

The world slowed. He bent his knees and put both hands under Kix's arms. His silver pistol pointed straight into the air, the barrel no longer aimed at either of us. Fatal mistake.

My hidden left hand rose into view, revolver gripped tight. I spun the Kimber back into my grip and swung my right arm forward.

He launched Kix at me, not realizing how difficult throwing a twenty-pound object would be. His throw only propelled Kix a foot over his head and four feet forward.

I surged toward him in slow motion. I refused to let Cannon's last act on earth be cracking Kix's head on the sidewalk.

He leveled his gun at me. I squeezed off two shots with the revolver in my left hand before I brought the Kimber to bear with my right. I fired again, four more shots with each gun, yanking the triggers so fast the gun blasts sounded like a machine gun. Ten shots total. The sharp crack and muzzle flashes were disorienting in the downpour. But I didn't miss.

My hands released the weapons and I dove forward, arms outstretched. Kix landed on my forearms as I hit the cement, cushioning his fall. My jaw hit the ground hard, and bells rang in my head. My son rolled forward out of my grip. Dazed, I grabbed at him but missed. In my fingers I held only the tape which used to be around his mouth.

The pistols clattered to the ground on each side of me, and Cannon fell like a sack of wet sand.

Free from the tape, Kix began crying. I peered through the pain at Cannon. His body lay still, his gun several feet from his hand. He was dead.

Kix army-crawled forward to me, his face pitiful and scared.

I reached out and picked him off the ground before Cannon's blood, diluted and spreading quickly in the falling rain, reached him. More blood on the school's sidewalk. At least it wasn't ours. Rolling over onto my back, I laid Kix on my chest, facedown, and let him cry.

"You crawled." I smiled. "Daddy's proud of you."

51

No matter how many flowery wallpapers they try, hospitals will always be depressing places. I sat on a chair with my head in my hands. I hadn't slept in thirty-eight hours. Kix lay in bed beside me, a machine monitoring his heartbeat. His chest rose and fell, and every few minutes he'd take a deep breath and shift underneath the pressed white sheet. The halls were quiet; visiting hours were over. I'd turned the lights off but the door to our room was open and a nurse walked by periodically. Rain beat silently on the window. I'd only recently dried out, and I still kept the blanket around my shoulders.

Detective Andrews arrived, soft footfalls. He stood framed in the doorway, looking at Kix.

"How is he?"

"He's good," I said. My voice was hoarse. "Cannon overdosed him with some kind of sleeping medicine. They pumped his stomach to be safe, and they're checking his blood. But he should be fine when he wakes."

Andrews sank into a chair opposite me and rubbed his face.

"Got a call from people across from the school, saying they heard gunshots. What else is new," he said.

"You'd think by now they'd be used to it."

"We found Cannon, or what's left of Cannon, some duct tape, and three guns. Now we're really confused."

"Rookies. Can't read the clues."

"Then the dispatcher calls on the radio. Says Leta High called 911, said someone kidnapped Kix. So now I know most of the story."

"Cannon is your killer. One of the revolvers is mine, the .38. The other will match the one you're looking for. I found Cannon at the school after Leta told me Kix was taken. He told me he killed Allen and Davis to discipline me, remove distractions."

"So he was obsessed."

"Yes."

"Then you shot him," he said.

"Yes."

"One hundred times."

"I lost count." No I didn't. Ten times. All hits. I could still hear blasts in my head. "I was a little emotional. He had a gun on Kix."

"Man."

"Yeah, it was awful."

"So the Murphy drug bust? Cleaning parties?" he wondered aloud.

"Catching Murphy was a bonus, but had nothing to do with the homicides. The cleaning parties appear to be legit. They just happened to be a good excuse for Cannon to catch victims at school late. Cannon was pretty good with computers, and I bet his machines will divulge how he accessed emails."

"Sounds like you got it all figured out."

"I'm pretty amazing," I sighed and looked at my son on the hospital bed.

"I'll get an official statement from you later. Need anything?" He stood up and paused at the door.

"Keep press out of the hospital."

"Done." He left.

I punched in a number on my cell.

"Bingham," he said.

"Cancel your plane ticket. I got him."

"About time," he said. I could hear hidden relief on the other end.

"Agreed."

"You said 'him.' Who was it?"

"Watch the news tomorrow. I don't want to spoil it," I said.

"I'll tell Anne. She'll be relieved."

We hung up. I thought about eating some of the soup and sandwich someone brought from the cafeteria. But I couldn't move. The love seat against the far wall looked comfortable but it was so far away.

KIX'S LAUGHTER woke me up. I pried open an eye and saw Mr. Suhr bouncing an Elmo doll around on the bed.

"You're ubiquitous," I croaked.

"What does that mean?"

"Seemingly everywhere,"

"You English teachers." He grinned.

"What time is it?"

"Seven in the morning. A lovely lady named Leta brought you some sausage and egg biscuits."

"She's the best," I said. "And you're not so bad."

"Your son's tests came back. He is clean, and he can go home."

"No school today?" I asked.

"No school today."

"I bet Gee is tired of cleaning blood off the sidewalk," I said.

"The Lord was with you, Mr. August."

"Doesn't feel that way in the hospital with my drugged son."

"It could have been much worse, and the evil has been extinguished. Looking back, you will see God moving more clearly. It is hard to see in the moment."

I stood up from the couch. Apparently I'd sleep-walked in the night. I stretched out my knotted muscles and crawled into bed with

Kix and a biscuit. Kix pointed at the biscuit and smiled at me. I'm a pushover, so we shared.

"Cannon was a Baptist. Baptists are the worst."

"I'm a Baptist. And I do not know the whole story," he said. "But I would guess Mr. Cannon was imbalanced mentally. Certainly spiritually."

"Press outside?"

"Some, yes." He held up a newspaper. "Would you like to read about yourself?"

"Not really. Summarize it for me," I said around a bite of sausage.

"Mr. Cannon has been identified as the suspected murderer of Mackenzie Allen and Roy Davis. He stole Mack August's baby, and so the Fighting Father killed him."

"Does the paper mention I'm a few pounds over my fighting weight?" I asked.

"It does not."

"Whew."

~

Andrews called me at home later that day. Kix and I were eating sherbet and watching Sesame Street. He'd earned it. Every few minutes he'd look up at me and smile. I'd earned it too. Outside the rain had stopped and the aching in my jaw was subsiding. Life was good.

"Good thing you got Cannon when you did," Andrews said.

"You search his house?"

"Yes. One whole freaky room dedicated to you and the murders. Looks like Taylor was going to be next."

"When?"

"Dunno," he said. "He had something of a running diary. It includes notes on Allen and Davis, and he started taking notes on Taylor. Bible verses everywhere."

"What's the diary say?"

"Haven't read through it all yet. It mentions you getting the eighth-grade teaching job instead of him, contains a list of your sins, monitoring your emails. That sort of thing."

"I'll come take a look later."

"You know," he said. "Maybe you better not."

"Why's that?"

"Take my word for it. It's probably just better you don't."

"Yikes," I said and my imagination took off. Pictures of Kix and me? Pictures of us sleeping, maybe? The thought of him in our house, sneaking around with a camera, was disturbing. I decided I didn't want to know. "Yeah, okay."

"We boxed the really freaky stuff. Don't want it leaked. And get this, I got a call from the former manager of a taco joint, down in North Carolina. He saw Cannon on the news and looked me up. A few years ago Cannon worked for him, and one of the other employees went missing. The manager and the police always suspected Cannon, just never had any proof. Never found the body."

"Might turn up in the diary," I offered.

"Yeah."

"Should make for some nice reading tonight. Cozy by the fire."

"You're sick."

"But I'm alive."

"Listen, Mack, I really appreciate your help on this. Cannon was a ticking time bomb, and he wasn't even on our radar screen. This could have gone on a while without us finding him. For a big city cop, you're okay. A lot of people owe you," he said.

"You're probably right. Tell the sheriff that he's welcome."

I STARED BLANKLY into the fridge, wondering what to do for dinner. Our supply ran low. Ms. Allen had sent over a basket full of fruit and cheese, and a card, earlier. Too tired to cook, I was considering a fruit, cheese, crackers, chips and salsa night when the front door opened and Taylor Williams stuck her pretty head in.

"If you let me come in," she said, "I'll let you have some of the beer and pizza I brought."

"I can't say no," I said.

"If only that were true," she sighed. She wore pink heels, a khaki skirt that swished around her knees when she walked, a pink button-up cotton top, and her hair was held back with a pink headband. She moved like she was on display, deliberate steps with her long legs. I didn't think I'd be able to say no tonight. I was exhausted, physically and mentally. I was lonely, and company in bed sounded too good. Never let yourself get too hungry, angry, lonely or tired, otherwise you'll do something you'll regret. Now that Kix was safe again, I wasn't really angry, but still had three out of four going.

Pizza never tasted so good. Kix banged on his tray, stuffed pizza into his mouth, drank milk and laughed during dinner. He needed a mom. Taylor talked about how she never guessed Cannon, and recalled the first time she met him.

"So," she said after a while. "I'm here to tell that I'm done chasing you."

Darn it. Just one more day.

"Whew," I said.

"Right." Could she tell I was close to caving? I drank more beer quickly. "I've realized that I'm in a place in my life right now where I feel like I just need to grow up a little bit. Do you know? I've been doing a lot of thinking about me, and I'm unhappy with myself. First things first, I'm going to stop chasing men. Specifically, you. If you decide you want me, you know where I live."

I nodded.

"So I bought a yoga DVD and a book on envisioning your way to success."

"You think stretching will help you find yourself?"

"It's more than stretching." She scowled. "Okay, smart guy, what do I do?"

"What do you mean?"

"I mean, Jesus, Mohammed, Buddha, the Dali Lama, Ghandi, Tom Cruise. What do I do?"

"Can't believe Tom Cruise made that list," I said.

"What? He does stuff like that."

"I was a wreck, Taylor. Hurting everyone. Too messed up to consider being a Hindu; I'd come back reincarnated as a frog. My mind was too sick to empty it and be a Buddhist. I was tired of violence and I didn't want to follow Mohammed. I didn't want to pay money for my salvation or the salvation of my relatives, so I didn't follow Joseph Smith or Tom Cruise."

"So what?"

"Jesus seemed like the only guy who'd like me."

"You sound like a terrible priest."

I sighed. "I'm not a priest."

"You're a hot priest."

"Well, you may be right."

"Fine. I'll get a book on Jesus too."

"I won't tell you how it ends."

"You've read the whole thing?" she asked.

"The Bible? Hell no. I suck at this."

"So can we be friends?"

"Probably not," I said.

"What? Why not?" She pouted, and it was an elite pout.

"Williams, you're so hot that I don't know where to look. And you're so wrong for me that if I gave in to you then it'd kill me cause I wouldn't be able to stop. So we'll be coworkers and I'll admire you from afar and try not to think about you at night. But that's it."

"What's a girl to do with so many underhanded compliments?"

I shrugged.

"This isn't fair." She kept pouting.

"Tell you what. Without looking, tell me what color Kix's eyes are. If you guess right, I'll take off my pants this instant."

"Brown," she beamed. "Just like yours."

"Clear blue, like his mother's."

"So what? Why is that important?"

"Because Kix is the most important thing in my life," I said. "And to you he's a distraction. I killed the last person who called him a distraction."

"Literally?"

"Shot him ten times."

"What's it like killing someone?" she said.

"Not fun."

"Maybe I can help you recover. Back massage? Front massage?"

"You said you were going to quit this."

"Old habits." She smiled. "You're worth it."

EPILOGUE

In April, the administration handed out Intent Forms for teachers to declare whether they'd be returning for the next school year.

Kix and I were going to move to my old home Roanoke, the fourth largest city in Virginia, and home to several big inner-city schools that could use a guy like me. Surely nothing could go wrong there.

I wrote "Hell No" on the form and turned it in.

Mackenzie boys, going home.

∼

ENJOY THE BOOK? (You did) Read more Mackenzie here! There are 6 books in the series, so far.

SIGN UP for my newsletter here. I alert you about my releases, and always offer new books at a discount for my email list.

AUTHOR'S NOTE

Hello!

Fun fact - this was the first novel I wrote, and I didn't plan on releasing it. But I love Mackenzie so much that I went back, patched it up, wrote a sequel, and released. You will probably note an improvement in craft in *August Origins* and the rest of the series.

Many thanks to my parents for letting me write on their computer for so many hours and for so many years, circa the '90s.

Thank you to my test readers - Matt Rawls, in particular.

Thank you to my lovely wife Sarah for indulging dreams.

www.ingramcontent.com/pod-product-compliance
Lightning Source LLC
LaVergne TN
LVHW040057300325
807160LV00002B/166